PISTOLS

AND

POINSETTIAS

A Smiley and McBlythe Mystery

PISTOLS

AND

POINSETTIAS

A Smiley and McBlythe Mystery

BRUCE
HAMMACK

1

___

"Are you over being mad?" asked Heather.

Former homicide detective Steve Smiley waited for the boarding announcement to end before he answered. "I'm surprised, not mad. It's not every day a washed-up cop gets asked to speak at a mystery writers' conference. I'm glad you gave me a few days to gather my thoughts."

"No problem, partner. Put your hand on my shoulder, we'll be the first to board."

A white cane with a plastic tip led their way down a long gangway to a Miami-bound Boeing 737. Steve mumbled as they escaped the terminal, "At least I can get away from that stupid Christmas music."

Heather scooted into a first-class seat by the window, leaving Steve to ease into the aisle seat. He folded his collapsible cane into one-foot sections and stuffed it in the seat pocket.

"You never told me the name of the group we'll amaze with our brilliance." said Steve in his tongue-in-cheek tone.

"Perhaps I should wait until the cabin door is closed."

"Uh-oh. This sounds like a trap. Why couldn't you have found me a nice murder to solve? You did such an outstanding job last year; I almost forgot it was Christmas."

Heather ignored the comment. "We're conducting workshops at the Women's Mystery Writers Association, or WMWA."

Steve dragged a thumbnail over his clean-shaven chin. "No men?"

"A few tokens."

"Great. You're throwing me into an estrogen-enriched environment with women writing about suspicious deaths in bookstores and tearooms."

Heather cut her emerald eyes to look at him. "Was that a sexist remark, Mr. Smiley?"

He continued with a deadpan expression and switched to a 1940s film noir gangster voice. "Take it any way you want, Toots. I'm partial to dames, as long as they keep the seams on the back of their hose straight."

Heather had picked that moment to take a sip from her Starbucks cup. Coffee almost came out of her nose.

Passengers continued to file down the aisle. The bump on the back of her seat told Heather the two women who passed had taken their places behind them.

A voice laced with sarcasm sliced through the din. It came from the woman seated behind Steve. "There she is, our illustrious president. Not flying first class, Hazel?"

Heather had to look around Steve to see the reaction of the elderly woman in the aisle. She stopped as the line to the back of the plane jammed like cattle in a chute. The silver-haired woman corrected her posture the best she could while leaning on a silver-handled wooden cane. Casting her gaze to the source of the question, hooded eyes flashed as she spoke. "If you find it necessary to address me, use my namme. It's Mrs. Smallgrass, and I'll address you as Miss Lutz."

"Make that *Ms.* Lutz. Miss is so outdated." She paused. "Although, I suppose I should make allowances for your advanced age."

The elderly woman's chin raised. Her voice held the edge of a rusty steel knife, old but still capable of serious injury. "*Ms.?* I read recently that Ms. came into vogue for women incapable of attracting a husband."

The next words came like cold honey, slow and sugary-sweet. "No, Hazel. Your memory is slipping again. Ms. is what we call women who aren't living in the nineteenth century."

"My memory is good enough to remember what you were before you attempted to become a writer."

The reply came quick and hard. "I hope you can remember what you or your people did with Kira Kelly's body."

The line moved, but not fast enough. The younger of the two women added, "You'd best run along to the cheap seats. Perhaps your next book will sell enough that you can afford an upgrade."

Heather peeked and covered her mouth with her hand. The aroma of coffee drifted through first class as brown liquid dripped from the nose and chin of the woman sitting behind Steve.

Accusations and counter-claims flew like colored confetti.

The elderly lady answered the last comment with a saccharine-sweet denial of any intentional wrongdoing and resumed her trek toward the back of the plane. Ms. Lutz, sitting behind Steve, asked an attendant to bring her a rag.

A sigh of satisfaction came from Heather's right. Steve leaned into her and whispered, "After four months without a case, it's good to hear a cat fight. If those women are going to the writers' convention, this trip has potential."

It didn't take long before the pilot throttled up. The plane splashed its way down the runway of Houston's George Bush International Airport, gained speed and tilted skyward. The mood among the passengers rose with the aircraft. Cold, wet, early December weather gave way to bright sunshine as soon as the plane bumped and shoved its way through the blanket of steel-gray clouds.

Heather leaned her head back. Steve had joked about the conference having potential, his way of sensing trouble and making light of it. Could this be the beginning of a reprise of last Christmas's murder investigation? Not likely.

She accepted a flute of champagne and went back to her musings. The dispute between the elderly woman with the unusual name of Smallgrass and Ms. Lutz had the markings of mutual disdain. No. It went deeper. She took a sip and dismissed her thoughts. After all, how much trouble could a group of introverted writers get into?

2

———

A red light flashed. A buzzer gave off a rude triplet of alerts. Bags, suitcases and various types of steerage spit out of an opening and onto a carousel. Heather joined the throng waiting to claim luggage as Steve stood a safe distance away from the scrum.

The recipient of the coffee shower, Ms. Lutz, pushed a large hard-sided suitcase toward Steve. Heather almost missed their bags, but snagged all three before they made another lap. She wrestled them from the merry-go-round and maneuvered her way through the mass of humanity. Whoever thought to put wheels on suitcases would have her eternal thanks.

Steve stood like a rock amid a rushing stream of people. He wasn't a large or exceptionally handsome man, but he could charm when necessary and exuded a quiet confidence. At five feet ten and a few ounces shy of a hundred and ninety pounds, he could stand to spend more time on the treadmill. His brown hair hadn't received a decent haircut for as long as she'd known him. He steadfastly refused to patronize any place but Tim's Barber Shop, a bastion of manhood where the flags of the armed services hung proudly on the wall. She went with him once and felt as welcome as the first female reporter allowed in a pro football team's locker room.

By the time Heather braved her way through the fast-moving crowd with their luggage, Ms. Lutz's suitcase lay open at Steve's feet, where she sifted through neatly packed clothes. A searching hand retrieved a flowing, floral wrap-around skirt. She dug further and harvested a color-coordinated aqua-marine knit top. Holding them up for inspection, she said, "These will do."

Fashion-model looks stretched from Ms. Lutz's raven hair to her pedicured toes. Violet eyes shone through lashes that defied natural length. The lightness of her complexion showed she wasn't a sun-worshiper, which played to her advantage. The contrast between her ebony hair and milk-white complexion gave the woman an air of mystery. Chest-length waves fell over her left eye, giving her a sultry peek-a-boo look.

"Be a dear and stand by your husband," said Ms. Lutz. "I don't like to show my wares unless I'm being paid for it, and that was some time ago when I modeled." She paused and cut her eyes in Steve's direction. "He's blind, isn't he?"

"Blind but not deaf," said Steve. "I take it you're getting out of coffee-stained clothes before you take your followers to the writer's convention."

"An observant blind man. How unique. I need to jot that down and use it in a future story."

Heather's eyes opened wide when Ms. Lutz wrapped the floor-length skirt around her waist, then reached up from the bottom and unbuttoned her skinny jeans. Quick as a blink, she'd shrugged out of them.

Ms. Lutz's eyes narrowed. "You two were sitting in front of me, weren't you?"

"Guilty," said Steve.

"That means you eavesdropped on the little fracas I had with Witch Hazel. You naughty man."

Steve stuck out his hand. "I'm Steve Smiley," he tilted his

head to the left. "This is Heather McBlythe. We're here for the writers' conference, too."

Heather stuck out her hand and received a greeting from the woman who seemed oblivious to people staring at her.

"I don't recognize your names. Are you writers?"

Brushing against Steve's arm, Heather tried to provide a curtain of sorts as Ms. Lutz's pencil-long fingers undid the buttons on a cream-colored blouse. Before Heather could do anything but gape, Ms. Lutz stood in her bra with a knit shirt in her hand. She made no move to put it on.

Heather found her voice. "We're not writers. We're here to teach."

Keen eyes bore into Heather. "I didn't see you on the schedule. What will you teach?"

Heather glanced around to see how many people were staring and moved tight against Steve. "We're last-minute additions. Mr. Smiley is a former Houston homicide detective and is now my partner in our private investigation firm. I'm an attorney and will give tax tips and answer questions about my time as a detective in Boston. Steve will give a demonstration on interrogations and extracting confessions. Together, we'll hold a question-and-answer session on what it's like to be private investigators specializing in murder cases."

Steve took up where Heather left off. "We team up from time to time to work on cases that interest us."

The woman's eyes widened. "I knew I'd seen you two. You solved the Blake Brumley murder last Christmas and helped Bella find her birth parents. Isn't that being made into a movie?"

Heather nodded. "The only thing slower than the justice system is Hollywood. They've pushed back the release date."

Any further discussion would have to wait as three soldiers in camo uniforms slammed to a stop and stood frozen in full ogle. Aware of their attention, Ms. Lutz turned and issued a dazzling smile. "My top goes on in ten seconds. If you can't get your phones out and take the picture by then, you're out of luck."

After the allotted time, the deep-cut knit top slid over one of Frederick's creations and she handed each man a business card. "Go online right now and download my first book. It's free and I guarantee you'll want to purchase the entire series." She sealed the deal by giving each a kiss on the cheek and thanking them for their service.

Her smile left as soon as the men turned to leave. By this time, a group of women had gathered around them. Ms. Lutz turned to them and barked out, "Always be looking for opportunities to sell your books, ladies. If each of those soldiers follows through and purchases my entire collection, I'll sell sixty-six books." She pointed toward the exit. "There's a shuttle to take us to the hotel. Let's be first to get checked in."

Her gaze fixed again on Heather. "Please join us. My name is Elissa. There are so many things I have to ask you and your husband."

"The only things we share are an occasional murder and Heather's cat, Max," said Steve. "I'm a widower and Heather is in a steamy relationship with a man she calls her stud-muffin."

Heather gave him a good-natured sock in the arm while Elissa flashed a smile brighter than the Miami sun. She scooped up her discarded clothes and pitched them in the trash. The wheels of dozens of suitcases and travel bags clickety-clicked as they rolled toward the door. Humidity and bone-warming sultriness hit them as soon as they left the terminal.

THE SIXTEEN-PASSENGER PEOPLE MOVER FILLED WITH VOICES and luggage. Elissa motioned for Heather to put Steve in the first of three seats that faced the bags. Heather took the next seat with her back to a window and Elissa sat next to her. A modern remake of *The Twelve Days of Christmas* streamed from overhead speakers. Steve let out a low, mournful groan. Elissa leaned over and whispered in Heather's ear. "What's wrong with him?"

By cupping her hands, Heather formed a miniature sound barrier. "He hates Christmas. Carols, hymns and music set him off."

Heather looked over her shoulder and noticed a group of women gathered on the sidewalk as they pulled away from the curb. Hazel, the airline coffee thrower, stood in the middle of fifteen-or-so women, luggage gathered around their feet like chicks around mother hens. Smiles were few among the ladies left waiting for the next hotel shuttle.

They hadn't traveled far when Steve turned and spoke Ms. Lutz's name.

"Please, call me Elissa and I'll call you Steve."

He nodded. "Elissa, I know nothing about writers' groups or their national conventions, but isn't the first weekend in December an odd time to be holding it?"

A burst of disgust came forth. "We can thank our illustrious president for this. She claims the Gaylord Hotel in Nashville canceled our September convention. I don't believe it."

"Why not?" asked Heather.

"This writer's group had its start in New York and spread from there. Many of the old guard still live in New England or have moved to retirement communities in Florida. By old guard, I mean traditionally published authors. Hazel wasn't expecting the rise of independent writers to become so popular."

She caught her reflection in the window and smoothed her hair while not missing a beat. "Independent writers are spread all over the country, and Nashville would have been a more central location. We're to have our big election of officers at this year's convention, and Hazel will do anything to stay in power."

"I worked a case once that involved the murder of the president of a home-owner's association," said Steve. "It proved to be a hard case to crack because everyone hated her. I can see where writers would be passionate about their organization." His tone remained constant. "When you were having the discussion on the airplane with Mrs. Smallgrass, you all but accused her of something. What did you mean?"

Elissa dragged her teeth over her bottom lip and said, "I was looking for a reaction out of Hazel, and she didn't disappoint me. I don't want to discuss all the details here, but a woman who had an excellent shot at ending the reign of Hazel as president of our mystery writers' organization went missing four months ago. I suspect Hazel and her cronies of, shall we say, eliminating the competition."

Steve didn't react other than to say, "I believe I heard the name Kira Kelly on the airplane. Is she the missing woman?"

Elissa nodded.

Heather mouthed the words, "You need to speak. He can't see you."

"That's correct," said Elissa. "Kira is the most successful indie author in our organization."

The shuttle hit a pothole. Suitcases shifted and the ladies on the back row of seats went airborne an inch or two. After the squeals and excited comments died down, Steve asked, "What have you done to locate Kira Kelly?"

"I tried everything: phone calls, e-mails, text messages, you name it. It's like she's dropped off the face of the earth. Kira must have known something might happen. She gave me the name of a private investigator to call if she went missing."

Elissa turned her head, raised her eyebrows and stared. Heather waited for what she suspected would be next. "I was wondering, since you two are private investigators, would you look into Kira's disappearance?"

Steve nudged Heather. "Well, partner? What do you say?"

Heather considered the request. "I say we need more information before we commit to anything."

"I agree," said Steve. "Missing persons aren't our strong suit." He paused, "Unless they've been murdered."

Elissa's determination shone through. "Let's meet for dinner tonight after the happy hour. I'll bring the report from the private eye who looked into her disappearance. Perhaps you can see something he missed."

Something about the conversation didn't sit well with Heather. She shrugged and decided she needed to spend more time with Elissa to get a better read on her.

Steve changed the tone of the conversation. "We already have plans for dinner tonight. Bring a copy of the report from the investigator to happy hour and we'll study it. You'll have our answer in the next day or two."

For a moment, a spark of entitlement-laced anger flashed from Elissa's violet eyes. Heather concluded the willowy beauty wasn't used to the words, "Not now" or "No."

The people mover pulled into the hotel's driveway and Elissa brightened, showing two rows of perfect teeth. "I'll see you at the happy hour mixer. I'm sure we can come to an agreement after you've examined the report." She stood and addressed the women. "Here we are, ladies. Remember, the only way we'll succeed is if we vote as a block. Stay strong."

3

———————

The hotel dazzled with class, sophistication, and Christmas decorations. An ice sculpture of a slender man with a beak-like nose wearing a deer slayer cap sat boldly on a table in the massive foyer. Another ice sculpture caught Heather's eye. It portrayed a fisherman unhooking a lure from the mouth of what looked to be a trout. She scanned the length and breadth of the lobby and nodded her approval. Pots of poinsettias, so thick they looked like a carpet border, lined the walls.

Elissa continued to pepper Steve with questions while the ladies from the shuttle checked in and scattered to their rooms. With hours to go before the happy hour planned for five o'clock, some made plans to rest while others chattered about sunning by the pool, finding a real Miami mojito, or both.

A woman standing behind Steve had her head down reading a book. Not paying attention, she bumped into him.

"I'm so sorry, please forgive me."

"No problem," said Steve as he turned and faced the woman. He paused and sniffed, but not in a way anyone but Heather would notice. "How's that old book you're reading?"

A mouse of a woman looked up with wide eyes staring

through black-framed glasses, the lenses measuring two inches in diameter. She wore a blouse buttoned up to the neck, plain jeans and white tennis shoes. Her hair, the color of dirty sand, lay straight and flat around her face, while bangs brushed the top of her glasses.

"I'm so sorry, sir. I'm such a klutz."

Elissa broke in. "Steve, let me introduce you to Lara Lovejoy. Lara is the vice president of WMWA." She pronounced the acronym WUM-WAH.

With handshakes exchanged, Elissa asked, "How did you know Lara was reading a book?"

The line advanced and Heather had to reposition Steve before he continued. "I felt the V-shape of an open book on my back. I knew it was an older book by the unique smell, a little musty, but there's something else about it. Do you mind if I examine it?"

A worn copy of The Murders in the Rue Morgue pressed against the woman's chest, with only Rue Morgue visible through her hands until she placed it in Steve's outstretched hand.

As if reading braille, Steve ran his fingers over the cover, down the spine, and along the exposed ragged-edged pages. He put it up to his nose and took in a slow breath.

"Definitely an old book," he said. "I'm also picking up a faint smell of salt water. You must live on or near the beach somewhere."

"That's amazing," said Lara. "My condo overlooks the ocean and I love to read and write on the balcony."

Elissa took over. "Lara is the most successful writer in WMWA. She's won every award you can name, and you'll find she has the respect of everyone here, even if she is a trad."

The two women exchanged a smile of mutual respect.

Steve nodded but said, "I need an interpreter. What's a trad?"

"Don't worry," said Elissa. "You'll catch on to our lingo. A traditional author, or trad, is one who goes through the hassle of finding an agent, submits countless proposals and drafts to publishers and hopes against hope they're favored with a deal. Then, after they've been published, they realize the publishing companies take the lion's share of the profits for all their hard work."

"It's not as bleak as Elissa makes it sound," said Lara. "There are things about traditional publishing that are very appealing."

Heather wanted to pursue the conversation, but the line moved and Elissa faced the desk clerk.

"Reservation for Elissa Lutz."

Standing erect, but not tall, the man behind the counter nodded an affirmation that he had heard Elissa's name. Manicured fingernails with clear polish danced across a computer keyboard. "I'm sorry, Ms. Lutz, our records show you canceled your reservation. Unfortunately, the hotel is booked to capacity. If you'd like, I can try to find you a room in a nearby hotel."

Elissa leaned into the counter and locked eyes on the man who wore a light coat of foundation over his whisker-free face. "You've made a mistake. I did not cancel my reservation." She took in a deep breath and spoke through clenched teeth. "Get me the manager."

"Ma'am, I'm the assistant manager."

"Congratulations on being second best. Now, get me the manager."

"Before we bother Mr. LaPage, let me check the computer again."

An additional line opened next to Elissa, Steve, and Heather when another desk clerk arrived to speed up check-ins. A half-dozen ladies cued up.

"Reservation for Hazel Smallgrass," rang out a voice from the newly opened line.

Hazel turned to face Elissa and spoke louder than necessary. "It appears the child is having trouble living in a world populated with adults."

"It's nothing that concerns you." Elissa shot her an

accusatory glance. "Or does it? You wouldn't know anything about my reservations being canceled, would you, Hazel?"

"What a silly question. Are you sure you made one?"

No response came other than a suspicious stare.

"Was your credit card over the limit?" asked Hazel.

"Hardly. Unlike some people, I have books that sell."

Hazel signed for her room, took her plastic key cards, and left.

"That cow," whispered Elissa through gritted teeth. "She's behind this."

"I'm sorry Ms. Lutz, there are no rooms available and we do not record who calls to cancel reservations. This is the first time I've encountered something like this."

Elissa rested an elbow on the counter and leaned forward. "What are you going to do to rectify this? It's imperative I stay at this hotel during the conference."

He typed into the computer. "Normally it would be no problem to put you in another room, but we're completely booked."

Heather took a step forward and looked at the man's name tag. "Mr. Cruz. Are you positive? Every room?"

The man typed into the computer again. The look on his face told Heather what she needed to know.

"There's nothing I can give Ms. Lutz anywhere near the price range negotiated by the writers' group."

Heather had her credit card in hand. "How many bedrooms are in the Presidential Suite?"

The assistant manager perked up. "Three bedrooms, each with an en suite bath, a fully stocked bar, living room, dining room, kitchen, a separate office and a view of Miami Beach that is second to none. Maid service and a personal chef are available upon request."

Heather handed him her credit card. "Cancel the rooms for Steve Smiley and Heather McBlythe. Give one of those rooms to

Ms. Lutz. I'll take the Presidential Suite for the next four nights."

The man bowed and took her credit card. "I'll need to verify this charge. It should only take a minute. I'm sure you understand."

The conversation did not go unnoticed. Behind the assistant manager stood a middle-aged gentleman wearing the same suit worn by the assistant manager. Salt and pepper hair, parted on the left and cut close, contrasted against an ink-black thin mustache, a throw-back to 1950s movie stars.

In a deft move, the second man snatched the card from the assistant manager and handed Heather's card back. "The penthouse is yours, Ms. McBlythe, and let me express what a pleasure it is to serve you. I'm Brice LaPage, the hotel manager."

Steve turned toward Elissa. "Take me to the elevators. Things will move quickly from here on."

Heather and Mr. LaPage caught up with Steve and Elissa near a Christmas tree on the far side of a bank of elevators. "Don't worry about your bags, Elissa. They're being delivered to your room," said Heather.

With eyes narrowed, Elissa said, "I don't understand what's happening."

Steve responded in a deadpan voice, "This hotel is owned by McBlythe Enterprises. As a result, you have a room and I'm upgraded to the penthouse."

After rising several stories, Mr. LaPage handed Elissa a room key that looked like a credit card, bowed and wished her a pleasant stay. The ding of the elevator and the swish of the door preceded Elissa's departure amidst several expressions of gratitude.

Once the doors slid closed, the manager ran a plastic key card over a reader inside the elevator. "This elevator is the only one that services the penthouse. As you will soon see, it delivers you directly into the suite and not into a hallway. No one but you and approved hotel personnel have access."

As the elevator continued its ascent, Heather glanced down and noticed the manager's footwear. "Mr. LaPage, are those Allbirds you're wearing?"

A touch of pink came to his face. "Please forgive the informality. I know they look like glorified tennis shoes, but I'm recovering from bunion surgery and my podiatrist recommended I not wear tight leather shoes for another week or two."

A wave of her hand dismissed his explanation. "I've been meaning to try a pair; I hear they're comfortable, durable, and one of the most environmentally friendly shoes on the market. Do you like them?"

"If I had my way, I'd wear nothing else."

The doors retracted and Mr. LaPage led the way into the penthouse. "I'll have your maid unpack for you. She'll have instructions to press any clothes that might need it. If you desire, I'll send up a bartender."

"No need for the bartender," said Heather.

The man cast his gaze around the living room. "Oh, dear. I'm afraid the design crew hasn't been here to put up Christmas decorations. I'll send them right up."

"No!" shouted Steve and Heather at the same time.

Heather changed the strident tone. "That won't be necessary. Please wait until after we leave on Sunday."

"Very well," said the manager. "If you need anything, anything at all, call me."

The elevator door closed behind the man who acted as if he was ready to bow and scrape to Heather as if she wore a crown.

A bank of windows gave a view of Miami Beach and clear saltwater.

Steve searched the surrounding area with his cane. "Where can I sit?"

"Try the recliner two steps to your left. I'll take you around the suite in a few minutes."

Leather squeaked when Steve settled in a puffy-armed chair.

He folded his cane and placed it beside him. "What's the chances of this fancy place having a bottle of cold water?"

"I'd say excellent. There's a fully stocked bar, and unless I'm mistaken, the door by the bar leads to the kitchen."

She didn't have to travel far. "Glacier water, seltzer, mineral water or vitamin water?"

Steve shook his head. "I grew up playing outside and drinking out of a garden hose."

"Sorry, no hose water. How about Perrier?"

"Surprise me."

Heather raised her voice as she retrieved a bottle of glacier water from the refrigerator. "What did you think about Elissa's proposition that we help her find the missing author? What was her name?"

"Kira Kelly, and I'm having a hard time believing an elderly mystery writer like Mrs. Smallgrass is involved in anything like an abduction."

After wrapping the bottle in a paper napkin, Heather handed Steve his water. "Any other thoughts?"

"Elissa likes to be in charge."

"Do you think she made sure Kira Kelly isn't here?"

A simple rise and fall of the shoulders did and didn't answer her question. Steve let out a yawn, kicked off his shoes and raised his feet. "Let's have a talk with Elissa's nemesis at the mixer this afternoon."

"Hazel?"

Steve mumbled an affirmative answer through another yawn. "Sorry. Didn't sleep much last night."

"You never do from Thanksgiving until after the new year." She took a lap blanket from the arm of the couch and spread it over him. "You won't be worth a thing if you don't rest. I'll look around the hotel and be back in time to get ready for the happy hour mixer."

"Before you go," said Steve, "was Lara Lovejoy as much of a wallflower as she sounded?"

"Easily forgettable," said Heather. "In fact, I'm not sure I could give you a good description of her." Heather turned her head. "Why do you ask?"

"No reason. Take your time looking around."

If Heather knew anything about Steve, it was that he always had a reason for asking a question. What had she missed about Lara Lovejoy?

4

———————

"It sounds like we're walking into a gaggle of geese," said Steve.

Heather scowled as she nodded a greeting to a woman staring at Steve. A look of embarrassment passed over the mystery writer's face. People stared at those with physical or mental impairments without meaning to, but it irked her all the same.

Heather estimated the room, about the size of a football field without the end zones, easily held five hundred noisy souls. Many congregated near the entry doors, making it a chore to part the sea of bodies. Heather moved through the tangle of people with Steve's hand on her shoulder. His cane made narrow sweeps in front of his next step.

"We're in one of the hotel ballrooms," said Heather.

"What do you see?"

"Four to five hundred women are divided into two teams, with team A by the door and team B on the far side of the room. One by one, or in small groups, they break away and go to the bar in the middle. After they're served, they scamper back to their flock. Elissa wasn't kidding when she said the group was on the verge of civil war. It's dagger stares or gushy embraces for those coming to the cash bar."

"I'm always amazed at what people can find to fight over," said Steve with a wag of his head.

Walking into neutral ground, Heather said, "You look very smart in your new slacks and blazer. I need to make sure one of these ladies doesn't kidnap you."

Steve tugged on his jacket. "That would be a waste of any woman's time. As for the clothes, I had a perfectly good suit I could have worn. I think you forget I'm a poor widower on a pension."

Heather ignored his remark and guided him toward the most popular zone in the room. "Let's get something from the bar and mix and mingle." She stopped at the bar and asked him, "The usual?"

"Yeah."

She ordered a glass of Pinot Grigio that came in a squatty plastic cup and a non-alcoholic beer for Steve. She'd never pressed him to explain his decision to live virtually alcohol-free, but this wasn't the time to satisfy her curiosity. Eighteen dollars later, they left the bar.

Heather scanned the room. "Do you want to start with Hazel?"

"Sounds good. Let's see if she's half the witch Elissa says she is."

Weaving their way through the crowd, she navigated a path into the presence of the organization's president. The assemblage reminded Heather of ladies-in-waiting surrounding royalty.

Upon seeing them, Hazel raised her hand, and the gathering went silent. Each woman took a step back, then dispersed to an out-of-earshot distance where they reformed into smaller coveys.

Hazel took Steve by the arm with a hand that shook with a tremor. "I noticed you two on the plane. Let's have a seat and chat."

Heather noted the woman's countenance. Her eyes sunk into a face lined with age, while drooping eyelids gave her the appearance of extreme fatigue. Blue-gray irises, although hooded, held the flickering fire of determination. She reminded Heather of an aging prize fighter—near the end, but determined to go ten more rounds, even if it killed her.

They seated themselves almost knee to knee on chairs arranged in a triangle. With an air of aristocratic confidence, the president of the organization spoke. "I'm sure Ms. Lutz regaled you with tales of Witch Hazel. I hope you don't believe everything that minx told you."

Steve leaned forward. "Mrs. Smallgrass, we use an expression in homicide investigations. When someone casts blame on someone else, throw away ninety-nine percent of what they say and be skeptical of the rest."

The grand dame nodded her approval. "Well put, Mr. Smiley." She reached and put an age-speckled hand on his forearm. "Please call me Hazel. I loved my late husband, but I would have preferred his name to have been something a little less of a pastoral mouthful."

Steve placed his hand over Hazel's. "We've heard one side of the story. Tell us yours."

Hazel drew her hand away, folded it into her other and placed them on her lap. "I am a charter member of this organization. I've watched it grow over the last forty years. We've always prided ourselves on helping skilled women mystery writers succeed, and we believe professional agents, editors and publishers are the gatekeepers to quality publications. It's a question of the writer paying their dues and the cream rising to the top. We're also dedicated to helping unknown writers polish their skills, so reputable publishing houses receive quality submissions."

Heather broke in. "And then the internet came along and independent publishing changed everything. Am I right?"

Hazel issued a sigh. "Shoddy writers have flooded the market with millions of books that wouldn't make it past a middle school English teacher, let alone a professional editor. Anyone with a laptop can call themselves a published author if they pump out a few lines of nonsense, slap on a cover, and put it on Amazon. It's an industry that has gone from professional writers to hacks-with-Macs."

Steve leaned back. "Are you fighting windmills?"

She gave Steve an approving look. "I appreciate the quixotic reference, but I'm passionate about my profession and I'm intent on defending this organization from a hostile takeover by the Philistines of the writing world."

Heather asked, "Isn't there room for traditionally published writers and independents in this organization?"

"We accept both," said Hazel. Her gaze pleaded for understanding. "You can't believe how brash this new breed of writer is. Fame and quick fortune are their motivations while entitlement is their mindset."

Steve interjected, "Do you mean writers like Elissa?"

Hazel's body stiffened. "Especially Elissa. If she and those indie minions of hers gain control, this organization will go the way of so many church denominations. We'll split and form two impotent groups. One will strive to maintain high professional standards, while the other will abandon quality in favor of the modern version of pulp fiction." Her head dipped and shook. "No, that's not correct. Pulp fiction writers were much better."

Heather allowed a few seconds to pass while she digested what Hazel said. "What will happen this weekend?"

Pointing to the room, Hazel said, "Look for yourself. On this end we have our traditional authors. On the other end stand the young Turks. The numbers are evenly divided."

Heather noticed a third group formed in the center of the room, away from the bar. "Who's the group in the middle?"

"Those are the hybrids. They have contracts to publish through traditional publishing houses but also publish independently." She paused, looking tired and old. "You asked what will happen? We'll have the election of a new president on Saturday.

Normally, my reelection is a foregone conclusion, but I have health issues. With Kira out of the picture, they will nominate Lara to succeed me." She looked around the room. "I don't see her." She brought her attention back to Steve with a forlorn look. "I'm not convinced she has the mettle to stay the course. If this organization is to flourish under Lara's leadership, I'll need to guide her."

Steve tipped his head toward the other side of the room. "What about Elissa? Will she do everything in her power to become the new president?"

Hazel sucked in her cheeks, looking as if she'd tasted something rancid. "Unless Kira shows up. If that happens, it's anyone's guess who the next president will be."

Hazel cast her gaze first at Steve and then at Heather. Her voice dropped to a whisper. "The most vicious rumors are being spread that I am involved in Kira's disappearance. I'd like to hire you to find out what happened to her."

Steve didn't react outwardly, but then, he seldom did. In a calm voice he asked, "Why would you want us to find a woman who might defeat your candidate in the upcoming election?"

"Unlike most of the independent authors, Kira Kelly can write. Her stories show maturity of style, originality, and excellence that has made her a writer sought by many of the major publishing houses. She's a woman of exceptional energy and prefers to stay independent. I have found her to be level-headed, not a raging tempest like Ms. Lutz."

Steve shifted in his seat. "Has the organization made any attempts to find out what might have happened to Kira?"

Her head dipped and returned. "Our vice-president, Lara, is a thorough researcher. I assigned her the task of solving the riddle of where Ms. Kelly might be or what could have happened to her. She sought answers for a month and then took it upon herself to hire a private detective. Seven days and two thousand dollars later, he submitted a report. It concluded with a statement that there was no trace of Ms. Kelly. Poor Lara. She felt so bad about her failure."

Steve turned to Heather. "Have you heard enough?"

That feeling of excitement when the hounds prepare for the chase swept over Heather. Steve needed something to keep him occupied. It wasn't a murder, but anything would do, especially with Christmas music being piped into the room. Yet, she hesitated. "I'm almost ready. Hazel, we'd like a copy of the report from the private investigator. Once we examine how thorough he was, we'll let you know. Even if we do, there are no guarantees we'll find Ms. Kelly."

"I'll have Lara deliver a copy of the report to you."

"Tonight, if at all possible," said Heather.

The ever-practical Steve had another thought he directed to Hazel. "Who will be the next president of this organization?"

"I'll rally my troops and Ms. Lutz will rally hers. It promises to be a battle royal. The ultimate victory may well be in the hands of the hybrid authors."

Steve raised his glass in a mock salute. "To those who are about to die, we salute you."

Hazel bristled. "You may mock if you like, Mr. Smiley, but a suspicious disappearance has visited this organization." She passed her hand in the crowd's direction. "My life's work lay in the balance and I find it inconceivable that someone like Elissa would triumph over me."

Steve lowered his glass but didn't apologize for his words. Hazel described the power struggle in military terms. Battles cause causalities.

"I must go," said Hazel. She looked at the throng. "It's time to put on the hat of a politician and campaign."

Heather spoke up. "We're in the penthouse suite. Perhaps you could come up after this is over. It will be our pleasure to dine with you there, and we can discuss this further. Say eight o'clock?"

"I'll send Lara. I have sheep that are being tempted to wander from the fold. It promises to be a long evening for me." She looked around like a shepherd counting her flock. "Oh dear, I still don't see Lara. No matter. I'll send her a text and tell her to dine with you at eight."

5

———————

By the time Steve and Heather left the Grand Dame of the writers' group, Heather's wine had not only warmed, it had the flavor of a gym sock. She considered going to the bar to find something more palatable when a woman approached and blocked their way. Lines of worry etched the corners of the woman's mouth.

"Are you the two detectives that have everyone talking?" She gave her forehead a weak slap with her palm. "Sorry. That clumsy opening line didn't come out anything like I wanted it to." She extended a hand to Heather. "I'm Kate Bridges. Might I have a word with you? It's important."

Heather nodded as Steve turned his head slightly, something he did to hear with the better of his two sensitive ears.

"Would you like to go somewhere a little more private?" asked Steve.

"Please."

One of Heather's duties as Steve's seeing-eye assistant was to catalogue the appearance and bearing of people Steve might ask her to describe. Kate stood at five-foot-five inches. At about the same age as Steve, early fifties, she possessed a well-propor-tioned figure. The modest age lines radiating from her eyes and mouth didn't distract from her pleasant face. She held herself erect, but not stiff. Three quarter heels, pleated black slacks, and a taupe blouse looked to be of the highest quality, while a cashmere scarf of muted pastels draped over her shoulders. That touch of perfection sent a ripple of covetousness through Heather. The jewelry had the look of Cartier. Her hair shone in a well-styled shade of rich brown that ended at her collar. No sign of gray.

Having grown up around money all her life, spotting someone who wore clothes and jewelry the way Kate did was child's play. Steve wouldn't need to be told about the two-hundred-dollar-an-ounce fragrance. His keen sense of smell couldn't help but notice that touch of class.

Once seated, Kate worked her hands as if she needed to wash off a stain. "Thank you for seeing me." Her hand went over her mouth. "I'm so sorry, Mr. Smiley. That slipped out before I could catch it. Please forgive me."

The reply from Steve began non-verbally, with a laconic smile. "As a writer, you know language contains phrases that are easily misinterpreted if taken literally. I've never been partial to balancing a chip on my shoulder. Terrible things happen. That's life." He added, "That's twice you've apologized for things you didn't have to. Why don't you relax and tell us what's on your mind?"

An audible intake of air preceded a burst of words. "I want to hire you to find out what happened to one of our writers, Kira Kelly."

Steve's head bobbed, but only once. "You wouldn't be asking if you didn't suspect foul play."

"I don't know what to think. It's like Kira fell off the face of the earth." The hand wringing continued. "Her apartment in Chicago is vacant, and her cell phone went to voice mail before her inbox filled. I'm worried sick."

Heather interrupted. "Could there have been a family emergency? Or perhaps a romantic relationship swept her away."

"She has no family." Kate's countenance changed to a grin. Not a funny grin, more like one that tried to communicate, *You don't understand.*

"As for romance, Kira's first husband was an arrogant, womanizing, cocaine-snorting son of a prominent hedge fund manager. After three broken ribs she wised up, divorced the Neanderthal, and returned to her bubbly, happy self. Well, almost. The experience turned her off men. She gets all the romance she needs writing historical romance mysteries. She said there's no chance of receiving a ruptured spleen from a man who exists only in her imagination."

"You seem to know Ms. Kelly well," said Steve.

Her phone chirped the reception of a notification. "Excuse me. I need to respond to this." After her fingers tapped out a quick reply, she stabbed the send button and asked Steve to repeat what he'd said.

"Do you know Ms. Kelly well?"

"She's a doll and a darn good writer. We began writing around the same time and we critique each other's stories." She looked away. "Being an indie appealed to her. She could have gone with one of the big five publishers, but she believed being independent made more sense in the long term."

"What do you mean?" asked Steve.

"Indie writers who publish their own work have sole control over their intellectual property."

Heather added, "They keep the copyright on their books for the entirety of their life and their estate retains the rights for seventy years after their death."

"Ah," said Steve.

"Were the police contacted?" asked Heather.

The first response came out as a huff of disgust. "A lot of good that did. We're talking about Chicago, where murders are an everyday occurrence. It took me a week of phone calls before they did a wellness check. The police had the manager unlock her apartment, and they looked around. With no sign of foul play, the police lost interest before the door closed behind them. That's when I hired a private detective."

Heather's eyebrows went up. "I thought Lara was the one who hired a detective."

"She hired one first. When he didn't come up with anything, I decided to hire another one."

Steve remained stone-faced, his voice calm and measured. "And what did the investigator discover?"

"Nothing. He charged me fifteen hundred dollars to do a skip-trace and came up blank. He said there was no record of credit or debit card transactions after the day she disappeared. He claimed he did a bunch of other checks, but I think he took my money and ran with it."

"Do you have the report?" asked Heather.

"It's in my room."

"Hazel said she was going to ask Lara to dine with us tonight. Why don't you come too? We're planning to dine at eight."

"I'd love to." Kate's voice filled with expectation. "Does this mean you'll take the case?"

Steve chuckled. "Why not? I hear three's a charm."

"I beg your pardon?"

"It's an inside joke," said Heather. "We'll do all we can."

6

At six-thirty sharp, an olive-skinned man, with black hair piled on top of his head and secured in a man-bun, stepped off the elevator into the penthouse wearing a white chef's coat with baggy black pants and black crepe-soled shoes.

Heather rose from the couch to greet him as he wheeled a cart with enough food to supply a small village into the room.

Bowing slightly, he said, "Good evening. I am Raul and I will be preparing your meal this evening."

"It's a pleasure to meet you, Raul."

"Mr. LaPage has instructed me to prepare only the finest of the hotel's dishes for you this evening."

"That sounds very intriguing, Raul. We can hardly wait."

He inquired about food allergies then asked if others would join them. His hand went to his chin as he viewed Heather and Steve with an omniscient stare. Without another word, he spun on a heel and retreated to the kitchen.

Heather whispered to Steve. "Dinner may be a surprise, but I bet we're in for something decadent and delicious."

Steve quipped, "I'd prefer a chicken-fried steak with mashed potatoes and extra gravy."

"Not tonight. We're having proper food that isn't the color and texture of a cardboard box."

"My sensitive palate may rebel."

Pots clanged and Steve snored softly for the next hour and a half. He roused himself in time to go to his bedroom and came back to the bar with hair combed and fresh breath.

Heather made arrangements for Mr. Cruz to escort Kate and Lara to the penthouse. At eight sharp the elevator's bell dinged.

Heather rose to greet the visitors. Only Kate Bridges stepped out of the elevator. "Did Lara not come with you?"

"No, she sends her apologies. She had something come up that she needed to take care of. These conferences are a lot of work for the officers of the organization."

"I'm sure they are. Let's sit in the living room," said Heather.

Steve responded by walking a straight line from a barstool to a leather recliner.

Other than freshening her makeup, Kate looked the same as she did at the mixer. She took in the room's opulence and nodded her approval. Heather invited her to sit near Steve.

Raul came out of the kitchen with a silver tray balanced on his fingertips. He approached Heather and presented her with a glass of wine. "I asked the bartender at the mixer what you were drinking. He told me you tried a Pinot, but didn't come back for a second glass. I don't blame you. The hotel should be sued for serving it." He presented the crystal glass and waited for her to take a sip.

"Mmm. It's excellent, Raul."

He progressed to Kate. "I took the liberty and brought you the same as Ms. McBlythe."

A confident voice answered. "This will do nicely."

Raul made for Steve. "A non-alcoholic beer for you, Mr. Smiley. If you'd like, I can pour this into a glass or a frozen mug."

"No, thanks," said Steve. "The bottle works best for me."

Raul bowed and retreated to the kitchen.

Steve broke the silence. "Did you bring the report from

the PI?"

"Yes, I have them. Lara asked me to bring her report also."

Heather received the reports from Kate's outstretched hand. She guessed the length of each to be at least ten pages. Either the investigators had been thorough or they'd padded the reports with extraneous verbiage. Probably the latter, since neither one discovered the whereabouts of Kira Kelly.

Steve sat loosely in the recliner, but didn't recline. He eased into the evening by asking, "How long have you been writing, Kate?"

"I can't remember when I wasn't writing. It's all I've ever done and all I ever want to do. I was first published when I was fourteen." She looked down. "I should say I was first professionally published at fourteen. Before that, I wrote a one-page newspaper in elementary school. I guess you could say I have ink in my veins instead of blood."

"What's your opinion of independent authors?" asked Steve.

A manicured index finger ran around the rim of Kate's glass. "Traditional publishing has been very good to me. I get paid up front and then get a small commission on each book once sales cover the production costs by meeting minimum quotas. The publisher provides me with excellent editors. A staff of professionals also help with marketing and sales. To put it succinctly, they help me succeed."

Kate paused, and Heather wondered if Steve would press her to answer his original question.

Kate rewarded his patience by saying, "I have a thorough knowledge of how traditional publishing works, but that's not what you asked. You want to know why I also publish independently."

A spark came into her eyes. She leaned forward. "It's new and exciting to be the captain of my ship. I can write and publish as many books as I want and not have my agent or publisher tell me it may be a year or two before they're ready for release, if they release it all."

Steve asked, "What genre do you write?"

"Thriller and suspense. It's part of the mystery genre."

"That's a surprise," said Steve. "I'd have guessed you write cozy mysteries."

Kate scrunched her nose like a rabbit. "Not enough action. I wrote some cozies in high school, but I found they weren't my cup of tea."

Steve laughed. "Nice pun."

Her face turned pink. "I didn't intend to be funny. I know there's a niche for themed cozy mysteries, but I prefer to write stories with grit."

Steve's next question was the one Heather had been waiting for him to ask.

"What do you think happened to Kira?"

Brown hair swung side to side. "I can't imagine."

Steve cut her off before she could start another sentence, but his tone held compassion, not condemnation. "Yes, you can. You can imagine all kinds of things. You do it every day and then you put them down on paper with exceptional skill."

"Actually, it goes in my laptop," said Kate without being defensive. "But I understand what you're saying." She paused. "Yes, I could make up a hundred things that might have happened to her. But you're interested in facts, not speculation."

Steve countered with, "You know her; I don't. From what I hear, she's an excellent writer. Is she an impetuous woman, or shy and retiring? Paint me a word picture of Kira."

Kate lifted her eyebrows and puffed out her cheeks. "Kira's a city girl. Chicago. I find her to be bubbly and very much in love with life. She's about my size, but that's where the resemblance ends. When it comes to publishing, she's an all-in risk taker. It's hard to be an independent author and publisher if you aren't willing to walk out on a limb. She's also very smart. She studies the latest trends in publishing and is up-to-date on all the recent tech stuff."

"You refer to Kira in the present tense. You must think she's still alive," said Steve.

"I can't bring myself to think the alternative."

Heather broke in. "You said Kira takes risks. Does that mean you think we should check out large cities or should we look on tropical islands? Perhaps she got over her aversion to men and she's enjoying a walk on the wild side."

Kate's smile seemed to brighten the room. "I don't think you'll find her lounging on a South Seas atoll with tall, tattooed and sun-bronzed." She paused and stared across the room for a moment. "That would make a splendid story. The heroine has amnesia and the guy who hit her with a crowbar tells her she's his wife. He's a low-life with plenty of ink and scars, perhaps an eye patch. An FBI profiler tracks her down and saves her at the last minute."

She corrected herself. "Better yet, the evil antagonist gets the agent's pistol. Our heroine shoots him with a spear gun and saves the agent, the island, and possibly the world."

Steve slapped his thigh and let out a hoot of a laugh. "You have a great imagination. But why not send a blind private investigator to find her?"

Kate shook her head. "It wouldn't work, Mr. Smiley. In every story we ask our readers to suspend disbelief, but I'm afraid a blind detective is asking too much."

All three broke down laughing.

Raul arrived with a black bandana tied across his forehead. "Aren't we expecting one more?"

Heather looked at Raul and said, "We were, but she wasn't able to make it."

"In that case, if you'll make your way to the table, I'll serve you."

Heather frowned when her cell phone chimed. She didn't receive many phone calls at this late hour. A check of the caller ID brought a smile to her face that faded into wide-eyed concern.

"Bella? Where are you? Are you all right?"

7

At the sound of Bella's name, Steve stopped in his tracks. Heather punched the speaker option so Steve could hear.

"I tried to stop you earlier, but the elevator door closed before you saw me."

Steve's voice came out in a rush. "You're here in Miami? At the hotel?"

"Steve!" squealed Bella. Her voice had the timber of a seventeen-year-old with keys to a new car. "Yes. I'm here and I'm hungry. If you haven't eaten, why don't we meet downstairs in the Italian restaurant?"

"I have a better idea," said Heather. "Come to the penthouse and we'll eat here. In fact, dinner is almost ready."

"A restaurant sounds better than room service," said Bella.

Steve chuckled. "Heather threw her name around. There's a personal chef making it smell like a three-star restaurant up here."

"Yum. I'm on my way."

"Wait," said Heather. "I have to come down and get you."

Heather turned to holler for Raul. He stood four feet from her and bowed.

"We have an unexpected guest that will join us. Is there something you can whip up for her?"

He scoffed, "Raul does not 'whip up.' Raul prepares dishes that dance on the tongue." He raised his chin. "Describe to me our guest."

Heather took a breath and sprayed out a description. "Her name is Bella Brumley. She's seventeen, but as mature as any twenty-five-year-old."

Steve added, "You've probably heard of her or seen her on TV. She's been in front of a television camera since she was five. She used to star in a big game hunting show, but she switched to fishing this year."

"Any allergies?"

"None that we've discovered," said Steve. "She's partial to Italian."

"Say no more. Raul is always prepared. Salads will be served in twelve minutes."

Like a ghost, he disappeared. Unlike a ghost, he banged and clanged in the kitchen, making as much noise as a blacksmith.

"Steve!" Bella stepped out of the elevator and covered the short distance to the man who had found her biological parents.

Steve returned her hug and said, "You're dressed rather casually. Is it a fishing outfit?"

"She's here for the fishing expo. I should have known," interjected Heather.

Bella swung her waist-length braid of silvery-blonde hair over her shoulder and tented her hands on her hips. "Well, duh. What gave me away?"

She twirled for everyone to see her outfit. "How do you like it? It's the latest thing." Dressed in stretchy shorts and a long sleeve top that covered her arms to her fingers, she was a walking billboard of fishing brands.

Steve chuckled.

Bella's iceberg-blue eyes sparkled as she gave Steve another hug. "I've missed you so much, Steve. Why don't you spend

Christmas at my parents' resort again this year? Just because I'll be filming in Belize doesn't mean you and Heather can't go."

Heather swallowed. She'd committed to spend Christmas in Boston with her parents. Then, her romantic interest back in Texas had plans for the two of them for a New Year's celebration. She regretted leaving Steve alone at Christmas, but her mother and father deserved some of her time, as did Jack.

"Let me get back to you on that," said Steve. "Heather and I are working a case. I need to keep focused. If I think about tropical breezes, waves lapping to shore and sand between my toes, I won't be any good to anyone. Kate might fire us."

Heather took care of introductions.

"A case?" said Bella. "How cool. Is it another murder?"

"We hope not," said Heather. "A popular writer is missing. That's all we know so far."

Steve chimed in. "She's supposed to be here at the convention, but went missing a few months ago. So far, three people have tried to hire us to find her."

Bella screwed her face into a question and asked, "Three? That's suspicious."

Steve shrugged. "It's a first for me."

Raul opened the kitchen door, but only wide enough to declare, "Dinner will be served in two minutes. Please take your seats."

Bella scanned the rooms and hallways. "Where's the restroom? I haven't had a chance to take a break all day."

"First door to your right down that hallway," said Heather as she pointed.

Raul brought three chilled plates topped with a salad that would please the palate of any herbivore. He placed a ramekin of dressing beside the plates. "A strawberry and mango vinaigrette for the ladies and buttermilk-ranch and chive for the teen."

Heather dipped the tip of a spoon in the vinaigrette and popped it in her mouth. "This is fabulous." She looked at Steve as he tucked his napkin under his chin. "What about Mr. Smiley's salad?"

Raul shrugged. "The gentleman doesn't want a salad." He spun and left.

Heather considered calling Raul back, but Steve said, "He's right. I'm saving myself for real food."

Bella turned the corner from the hallway at the same time Raul came through the door, his gaze fixed on the fast-disappearing salads. He didn't see Bella until they almost collided. They avoided playing bumper-cars by holding out their hands. Each grabbed the other's forearms. Frozen in place, their eyes locked. Blue eyes stared into milk-chocolate brown, and vice versa, as both stammered out their apologies.

"Oh, boy," said Heather. "Here we go."

Kate chuckled quietly as Steve asked, "What's going on? It's awfully quiet."

"Hormones just burst into flames," said Heather.

"The cook and the fisherwoman?" asked Steve.

"They're in seafood heaven."

After several awkward moments, Heather rose and went to Bella. "Let's get you seated so Raul can tend to his duties."

It took a firm tug, but Heather broke the clutch. Bella, dazed like a boxer who'd taken a right cross to the chin, staggered to the table. Even while being seated, she kept her gaze locked on the kitchen door.

The sound of breaking china came from the kitchen, followed by words muffled enough those at the table couldn't make it out. It didn't take long before Raul pushed the door open and returned with a plate in each hand and one balanced on his forearm. With eyes fixed on Bella, he stumbled and did a spinning three-hundred-sixty-degree pirouette. Somehow, he used centrifugal force to keep the food anchored in place. His tan skin took on a rosy hue.

"Good save," said Kate.

He cleared his throat. "It's something you learn in culinary school."

Eyebrows raised. The exotic accent of the dazed man who used only one name had shifted to something you'd hear at a New York Mets game.

He regained his composure and his Latin accent. Placing a plate in front of Heather, he said, "For the ladies I've prepared seared bluefin tuna with wasabi butter sauce, a wild rice and quinoa pilaf, and grilled asparagus." He placed an identical plate of culinary perfection in front of Kate.

Moving on to Steve, Raul slid a plate in front of him. "For the gentleman, Breaded Veal Cutlet-Raul. It also is one of my signature dishes."

Heather took stock of the plate and exclaimed, "It's chicken-fried steak with mashed potatoes and green beans."

Raul tugged at his chef's coat and raised his chin. "Breaded Veal Cutlet-Raul is not a chicken-fried steak. The steak is from hand-selected Kobi beef, tenderized and re-chilled, but only after it received spices of my personal recipe. I then bathed the cutlet in pigeon eggs and goat's milk. I blend coconut flour with flour from unprocessed grains. Then, the meat is flash cooked in grapeseed oil. What you would call gravy is a sauce I make from heavy cream, drawn butter and arrowroot for thickening. The local, organically grown green beans add color to the dish. I hand select them and—"

Heather didn't let him finish. "I apologize, Raul. You're right. Breaded Veal Cutlet-Raul is not chicken-fried steak." She looked at the void in front of Bella. "Perhaps you should get Miss Brumley's plate."

Steve took his first bite, leaned back and moaned. "Raul's right, this is not chicken-fried steak. I don't know how I'll ever be able to eat at Dairy Queen again after this."

Raul looked at Bella and winked. "I've saved the best for you."

He jogged to the kitchen and returned with a silver pan the

size of a hubcap from a vintage Cadillac. He placed it in front of Bella and studied her face.

Heather looked at the creation and asked, "What do you call this dish, Raul."

"It's a New York-style pizza." he said with a return of his Big Apple accent.

Bella's face glowed with pleasure. "Perfect. Can you help me eat it? There's too much for me."

"That's a change," said Steve.

Heather surrendered and said, "Raul, you might as well get a plate and pull up a chair by Bella." She paused. "What's your real name?"

He looked down, seemed to summon his courage, and raised his chin. "Back in the Bronx they call me Robby, Robby Calano."

"Well, Robby," said Steve. "Heather has a problem that needs your expertise."

"I do?" asked Heather.

Steve put his fork down. "What can you tell us about the stealing that's taking place in the hotel's kitchens?"

8

―――――――

The Latin accent Robby brought to the penthouse fell away, replaced with something you'd hear on a subway or in New York's Central Park. "I can tell you a lot about what goes on in the kitchens of other hotels, but not this one." He looked up at Steve. "They hired me today."

"That doesn't help much," said Heather.

Kate asked, "Why did you feel it necessary to take on the persona of Raul?"

Robby lowered a folded slice of pizza to his plate. "When I went through culinary school, I noticed many of the top chefs are... how can I say this? Those guys, they're unique. They all do something to make themselves stand out. Multiple piercings, tattoos, wild hair and bizarre clothes. I'm new in Miami and I want to make a big splash. A nobody named Robby from a fourth-floor walk-up in New York isn't much to remember. My mom came from Puerto Rico, so I didn't have to fake the accent."

Heather pointed with her fork. "You don't have the hotel name embroidered on your chef's coat."

Robby shrugged. "Mr. Cruz, the assistant manager and Chef Miguel, the executive chef, interviewed me and hired me on the spot this afternoon. They seemed hard-up."

"How so?" asked Heather.

"They couldn't spare any of their chefs to cook for you because the hotel has all the rooms full of people here for conventions. That means the kitchens are crazy busy."

"Keep talking," said Heather. "This is interesting."

"What do you want to know?"

"How did they know you're a talented chef?"

"Chef Miguel grilled me for about ten minutes. He gave a nod of approval and I was in." Robby issued a smirk. "I think Chef Miguel plays the same game I do. I bet his actual name is Michael Schwartz, or something like that."

Steve pulled the napkin from the top of his shirt. "You didn't guess about what to cook tonight. How did you know what to serve?"

A sly smile pulled on the corners of Robby's mouth, and two deep dimples appeared. "Mr. Cruz told me big shots were staying in the penthouse. He wanted you wined and dined with the finest. I asked him who you were and about your background. That led me to call your office in Texas and talk to your receptionist. I laid my accent on thick. When she heard I'd prepare your meals, she opened up. She told me fancy seafood for Ms. McBlythe and chicken fried steak for you, Mr. Smiley."

Kate dabbed her lips with a napkin. "How did you pull the pizza out of thin air?"

Robby's smile broadened. "I have to eat, too. The hotel gave me a generous budget, and I thought, why not cook what I like? It was nothing but luck when I learned Bella's a pizza junkie."

Wide teenage eyes stared in admiration. "That's so clever." She turned to address Steve. "I think Robby would make an outstanding detective. Don't you?"

"Could be." He lifted his chin. "Robby, what reputation does this hotel have with food?"

He looked down at the remains of his pizza masterpiece.

"I've never eaten here, but I hear the restaurants are top quality."

"And the food for banquets and conventions?" asked Heather.

"Uh, not so hot. If you catch my drift."

"Be specific," said Heather.

He looked at Bella as if he needed her permission to be truthful. She nodded.

"The word on the street is it's a mixed bag. Sometimes it's fair, and other times you'd be better off at a fast-food joint."

Bella jumped in. "I can vouch for that. The fishing convention food tastes like..." Her chin dipped. "Let's just say what I had today wasn't very good."

"That means someone's cutting corners," added Robby.

Heather tapped her foot. "Anything else?"

Kate said, "I don't know where they found the wine for the mixer tonight, but I can't remember when I've tasted anything so rancid."

Heather nodded. "I thought my taste buds were off." She paused. "Now that I think about it, I didn't notice any hors d'oeuvres. That's supposed to be part of the convention package."

Robby stood to take up plates. "I'll be back with coffee and dessert in a few minutes."

"Before you go," said Steve. "It seems obvious there's something going on. We'd like to hire you to go around to the various venues tomorrow and give Heather a report of the quality of the food and the service."

Heather added, "Take photos if you can."

"Sure, no problem." The first word came out sounding like *shore*.

"I'll get the pictures," said Bella. "Robby and I can go from one conference to the next. We can pretend we're taking selfies." She rose from her chair. "Let me help with the dishes."

"You never volunteered like that when you were living with Heather," said Steve.

"I've grown up since then."

The two scooped up the plates and scurried to the kitchen while Heather contemplated how grown up Bella had become. Or soon would be, if Robby had anything to say about it.

A look of excitement crossed Kate's countenance. "This is fascinating, Steve. You and Heather now have two mysteries to solve. My head is swimming with ideas for plots and sub-plots."

Steve leaned back in his chair. "Let's hope the mysteries stay on paper."

Heather rose from her seat and headed to the kitchen. She opened the door and said, "Bella, could you come here?"

"This can't be good," mumbled Bella as she approached the table. "You used your mom voice."

Heather ignored the teen's complaint. "Are you staying in the hotel by yourself?"

"Uh-huh."

"Where's Uncle Olin? Isn't he still flying you and acting as your chaperone?"

"The plane needed one of its engines overhauled. He's staying at a hotel near the regional airport."

Heather placed her palms on Bella's shoulders. "We have three bedrooms. I want you to pack and take the empty bedroom here."

Bella squinted. Her gaze shifted and then came back with a look of hurt. "You don't trust me."

"Don't be silly," countered Heather. "We need Robby close and there are no empty rooms in the hotel. He can take your room and be near any time we need him."

Bella's eyes widened. "Awesome! I'll tell him."

The door to the kitchen swung shut as Steve leaned forward, his elbows on the table. "You sly woman. You know she'll be busy most of the days and evenings with her convention. By changing rooms, she'll be where you can keep an eye on her at night. That story about trusting her wasn't all the way true, was it?"

"I was seventeen once," said Heather.

"Weren't we all," said Kate with a sigh of remembrance. "Sometimes a little deception keeps small mistakes from becoming big regrets."

The evening ended with Steve in his chair, and Kate sitting close by on the couch, while Bella and Robby transferred Bella's things to the third bedroom. Heather took the reports from the private investigators and retired to her bedroom. She rose in time to see the party break up at eleven o'clock.

Robby cleared out to retrieve enough belongings for four days and nights. Kate hitched a ride with him on the same elevator, and Bella sang her way to a shower. Steve sat in the recliner with his index fingers steepled against his lips.

Heather slept well until 4:45 a.m. when her phone rang. She propped herself up with pillows behind her back and cleared her throat. "Hello?"

"Ms. McBlythe, this is Brice LaPage, the hotel manager. I apologize for the call, but there's been a serious incident here at the hotel and the police insist on speaking with you."

Heather looked again at the clock. "Why do they want to talk to me?"

The manager's voice sounded like it was being squeezed out of a juice press. "They're standing here and won't allow me to say anything more."

In the background Heather heard a testy voice.

"That's enough. Get this elevator moving."

9

―――――

Springing from bed, Heather slipped on yoga pants and a t-shirt and went to wake Steve. Still dressed, except for his shoes, he appeared as she'd left him, in the recliner with fingers steepled against his lips.

"I take it we're expecting company," he said in a monotone.

"Cops are on their way up."

The door to the elevator opened and out walked two men wearing khaki slacks and navy sports coats over pale blue shirts. The first out, a thin man in his late forties, took three quick steps, then grimaced before limping the rest of the way to where Heather stood. The second, taller, but younger by at least a decade and a half, followed in the first man's wake.

"Are you Heather McBlythe?" asked the leader.

Heather bristled and held out her hand, palm up. "Badges and ID's, please."

The staring contest lasted fifteen seconds. The elder man's puffy eyes, stubbled chin and scuffed shoes told Heather sleep deprivation accounted for part of his intemperate mood. Lack of sleep, however, didn't excuse boorish behavior.

The man broke the stalemate by jerking open a bi-fold case

from his pocket and flipping it open and shut in one smooth motion.

Heather pointed to the elevator. "This conversation is over. Show yourselves out."

Steve piped up from his chair. "I didn't catch your name, Detective. I can tell by your voice you had a long night. You should know the woman you're trying to bully is an attorney. Besides that, I didn't hear her toilet flush yet this morning." Steve pointed an index finger skyward. "Beware! Hell hath no fury like a woman with a full bladder."

Heather glared at Steve until she saw the corners of his mouth turn up. She directed her chilly stare back to the detective. "If you'll excuse me, I'll be back in a few minutes. By then, I hope your manners have caught up with you."

Steve dealt out introductions when she returned with hair and teeth brushed. "Heather, this is Detective Vance and Detective Warner with Miami homicide. I'm satisfied they're who they say they are." The static electricity in the air hadn't diminished.

Both men took a seat on the couch with Detective Vance sitting closest to Steve. Heather chose a wing-back chair across from them and settled in with legs crossed. She inspected the two men. Vance wore his salt and pepper hair slicked back, and his top lip sported a bushy mustache. His partner filled out his suit with a well-developed physique. She guessed him to have been a college athlete, most likely a running back.

Detective Vance scooted to the edge of the sofa and looked at Heather. "We understand a chef named Robby Calano was here last night."

"He's dead, isn't he?" asked Heather.

The detective narrowed his gaze. "Why would you ask that?"

Steve answered before she could. "Give us a little credit. Two homicide detectives arrive at four-thirty in the morning. What else could it be?"

"Yeah, Calano's dead. What do you know about it?"

"If you're talking about a murder, then we know nothing.

Everyone here was in by eleven o'clock. Where did it take place?"

"That's not important," said Vance. "Tell us what you know about him."

Heather took over. "This will go smoother if we exchange information. Mr. Smiley asked where this took place. That information will be on the morning news or I can call the manager and find out. We're both former cops, so we know what's important and what's not."

The two detectives exchanged glances. A nod of Vance's head gave Detective Warner permission to speak. "In the basement. The VIP parking garage."

Detective Vance didn't waste a second in asking, "What was he doing there?"

"There's an underlying assumption that we would know why he went there. We don't."

"Don't get cute, Mr. Smiley. This is a murder investigation."

"We've established that," said Steve. "What we haven't established is your level of competence in asking pertinent questions in a way that elicits useful answers."

"If you two don't want to answer questions here, perhaps you'd prefer a cozy interview room. One where we might not get to you for several hours."

"I'd think long and hard about that, Detective. Threats like that might be enough to get you an interview with a sour-faced internal affairs investigator. I'd hate to see you dig a hole you can't climb out of."

Steve leaned forward. "There's no need for this to be contentious. You play nice and we'll answer your questions."

Rubbing her eyes, Bella stepped into the room wearing sleep shorts and a ragged t-shirt with its tail cut off, exposing a pierced navel. "Is Robby here yet?"

Detective Vance sprung to his feet. "Were you with Robby Calano last night?"

She yawned and nodded before Heather could issue a warning.

Detective Vance withdrew handcuffs and closed the distance between him and Bella. "Hands behind your back."

Everyone came out of their seats. Steve issued a complaint over the detective's recital of the Miranda warning.

Heather blocked Vance's path. "I need to talk to my client."

He sneered. "Are you licensed to practice law in Florida?"

Heather looked around him. "Don't say a word to these men or anyone else. No matter what, don't say or do anything. I'll have you back in time for your show."

Limping to the elevator, Detective Vance passed Bella off to Warner who silently mouthed, "Sorry," as the door closed.

Heather sprinted to her bedroom, grabbed her phone, scrolled through a lengthy list of names and stabbed a number. On the fifth ring, a woman's voice crackled a weak hello.

"Wake up, Mindy. It's Heather. I need your help."

Leaving her bedroom ten minutes later, dressed in a black blazer with matching skirt and black heels, Heather expected to find Steve in the recliner, but he'd moved to the office. Ensconced behind the desk with his laptop in front of him and headphones on, he pulled them off when she entered. The room pulsated with a mix of anger and determination.

"Who'd you get?" he asked.

"An old Princeton buddy who's number two in the State Attorney General's office. She's calling all the right people."

Steve nodded his approval.

"What are you working on?"

"Background on Robby Calano. I'm not giving Vance the pleasure of solving this one."

10

———

The addition of a cart from room service marked the only change in the penthouse office when Heather and Bella returned.

"How is she?" asked Steve in a hushed tone.

Falling into a chair in front of the desk, Heather let out a huff. "Name an emotion. She let them all fly, along with enough tears to fill a lake."

"That's to be expected. Who told her?"

"Vance."

"I was afraid of that." Steve drew a hand over his chin. "He probably did it on the way to the station, trying to shock her into talking. Did Detective Warner play the good cop?"

"From what I could find out, Detective Vance ran the show by himself. I'll know more this afternoon."

Steve nodded. "Did you know Vance took a bullet in the leg nine months ago?"

Heather sat up. "You've been busy. What else did you find out about him?"

"He's clean and has a solid, but undistinguished, record. He's avoided internal affairs for twenty years. That's saying something these days."

Heather rose and stretched her fingers toward the ceiling. "I thought we were dealing with someone who didn't need to be carrying a badge. Why'd he act like such a jerk this morning?"

Steve lifted his shoulders and let them fall. "It could have been fatigue, pain, or something else. Is he still on the case?"

"I heard nothing to the contrary."

The office chair let out a squeaky moan as Steve leaned back and hooked his fingers behind his neck.

Heather took a long look at her partner. He kept his wits about him and sought more information while she went off as if a dragon needed slaying. She wanted to tell him how much she appreciated his calm demeanor and stalwart character. But she knew that wouldn't do anything but earn her a word or gesture of dismissal. Instead, she did what she knew he wanted her to do. "Where do we start?"

"Call the manager and tell him we need carte blanche with hotel security. If there's video of the parking garage, we might wrap this up before noon."

"I have a class to teach this morning and won't be available until that ends."

Steve rolled his fingertips three times on the desk. "I'll find someone to be my seeing-eye dog. But first, I need to talk to Bella. It seems there's a Mrs. Robby Calano in New York."

"He's married?" Heather stomped her foot.

"That's not all. Robby left behind a baby girl."

Heather threw up her hands. "I'm at full overload. Going to see a bunch of fussy writers will be a reprieve."

"I'll talk to Bella. It might take the sting out of lost love when she finds out her knight on the white steed had rusty armor."

SECONDS AFTER HE HEARD THE ELEVATOR DOOR CLOSE, STEVE picked up his cell phone and spoke a command. "Call Kate."

After the third ring, she picked up. "Steve, what a pleasant surprise. I'm walking into the convention. Are you already here?"

"Not yet. Heather's on her way, but it may be a while before I get there. I know this is an imposition, but something important has come up and I need someone to help me. Heather's scheduled to teach this morning and, well, I was wondering—"

"Say no more. Where do you want me to meet you?"

"First floor. At the elevators in the lobby in thirty minutes."

The pitch of her voice rose a third of an octave. "This is exciting. I'm to meet a private detective by the hotel elevators for something important. If I was writing this, the next line would be yours and you'd tell me someone's been murdered."

Steve stammered before he came up with something that would be truthful, but not shocking. "Keep working on the plot. It needs a few more elements to juice it up before something so dramatic happens."

The laugh reminded him of a mountain stream falling over smooth stones. His thoughts shifted to a distant memory. He and Maggie stood barefoot in a Colorado stream of melted snow. Rippling water laughed with them as they bet who could stand the numbing cold the longest. He lost his balance, and the bet, when he tumbled backward after a trout brushed his leg.

"Are you still there?"

Steve bit his cheek and stood. "Sorry. Yes. I'll meet you in twenty minutes."

"You said thirty."

"Yes. Thirty minutes. At the elevators."

On the way to take a shower, he wondered what triggered the memory of Maggie. Was it the laugh? Perhaps, but Maggie's laugh was like no other. His late wife didn't mess around when she laughed. It came from some deep place of joy and contentment with life. Kate's laugh had a pleasant ring, but lacked the *joie de vivre* of Maggie's.

A wave of guilt swept over him. What was he doing? There'd be no one who could take Maggie's place, no matter how pleasant her laugh, or how her perfume stirred something in him.

A second voice seemed to be speaking to him. A voice that told him to move on. Maggie's voice.

Once in the bedroom, he unbuttoned his shirt, stripped it off, and threw it in disgust. "If I don't do something about Christmas, I'll lose my mind again. This time I don't think I'll get it back."

Shaving in the shower saved time, and he still needed to talk to Bella. Under Heather's instructions, the maid arranged his clothes in the closet, left to right, pre-selected to match.

Ten minutes remained on his schedule when he knocked on Bella's door. He entered without permission. "Bella, I need you to sit up and listen to me."

"Leave me alone." Sobs came from what sounded like a face buried in a pillow.

"I can't leave you alone. I'm on my way to catch Robby's killer and I need you to listen to me."

The bedspread rustled. "Can I help?"

"Not yet, but I think I can use you later." It wasn't a lie. It wouldn't be a big assignment, but it could be important. He squared his shoulders. "I found out some things about Robby that I need to tell you before you hear them from someone else." He paused. "Robby had a wife and a daughter."

Silence fell on the room like a dense fog, but not for long. Steve hadn't realized how expansive Bella's vocabulary had grown, nor her penchant for throwing pillows. He escaped the room before her ire fell in his direction. He contemplated the mysterious fluctuations of a teenage girl's mind. Uncontrolled grief one minute and unrestrained fury the next.

With a few minutes to burn, he retreated to the recliner to think. The mystery writers' convention was turning out to be more than he expected. What else lay in store?

11

Heather wondered how Steve would handle Bella as she passed signs pointing the way to the various convention venues. She followed the ones marked WMWA and noticed Elissa standing outside the ballroom with a dozen or more women sporting identical scarves.

Elissa stepped into the aisle to intercept her. "Heather, good morning."

She returned the salutation and looked at a mound of cardboard boxes. "What's this?

"Something practical for the attendees." Elissa took Heather by the arm and led her to a table covered by an ample supply of scarves. "You know how cold some conference rooms can be. We thought it would be nice to give the ladies something to cover their necks. It also serves as a souvenir of the convention."

Heather took a scarf and unfolded it. It read: *WMWA: KEEPING PACE WITH CHANGING TIMES.*

Heather raised an eyebrow. "Is this the campaign slogan for indie authors?"

Elissa answered the question with a half-smile.

From the banquet room strode Hazel with a look of evil intent painted on her face. She paid no attention to Heather.

"Ms. Lutz, what's the meaning of this? Who gave you permission to distribute unauthorized merchandise?"

Elissa hugged her left elbow with her right hand. "Good morning, Hazel. Did you sleep well?"

"How I slept is none of your concern. Answer me. Why are you distributing these hideous scarves without permission?"

"Poor Hazel. How can one woman be wrong so often? You failed to trademark WMWA."

Hazel sputtered, "Everything related to Women's Mystery Writers of America is properly trademarked. I insist you pack these garish scraps of material and take them away."

Elissa took a step forward. "One more time, you've failed to do your job properly. Like I said, WMWA is not protected by a trademark, only Women's Mystery Writers Association. I noticed that you have used my trademark on several items. If anyone should remove their merchandise, it's you."

Hazel didn't give an inch. "The Women's Mystery Writers Association paid for this venue. We determine who can occupy this space, and you and your trinkets are not welcome."

Elissa pointed to the table next to hers. "The vendor who produces audio books sub-let this space to me. Nothing in the contract forbids them from sharing the space with another vendor or anyone they please. I split the cost and told them I only needed a small portion of the booth. They were more than happy to take me up on the offer." She paused. "Would you like to see the contract?"

Hazel looked at Heather. "Well, Ms. McBlythe, you're an attorney. What say you about this illegal infringement?"

Heather's hands went up to convey she didn't want any part of this disagreement. That didn't stop Hazel.

"Speak, Ms. McBlythe. Have I no recourse in this matter?"

Like being caught between two charging bulls, Heather had no place to go. No matter what she said, the wrath of one of the women would spew out on her. She called upon her upbringing and training to provide a diplomatic way out. Turning to Hazel she said, "Everything can be litigated, and it's possible you would prevail."

Hazel nodded like she couldn't wait to get to court. Heather let out a breath and took in another. "Unfortunately, this is a civil matter. If you call the police, they'll tell you to hire an attorney and file your case."

"I already spoke to an attorney," said Elissa. "She assured me you don't have a leg to stand on, and the convention will be over long before any judge would issue a temporary injunction for such a frivolous matter."

"I'm still calling the police."

Three clicks of Elissa's tongue sounded. "Poor Hazel. I have documents I can show them and I can be persuasive in ways you don't understand." The last statement carried with it the practiced look of seduction.

Hazel turned to leave. Unfortunately, she turned too fast. Hands stretched to hold her upright, but the best efforts of both Elissa and Heather failed. The matriarch of the writer's group went down in a heap.

She slapped away helping hands and lifted her frail body with the aid of her cane. Limping steps carried her into the ballroom.

Once Hazel was out of sight, Heather gave Elissa a disapproving stare.

"I know," said Elissa. "I was too hard on her, but that woman gives me a three-aspirin headache."

If she'd left it at that, Heather would have thought Elissa had a modicum of compassion. However, she had more to say.

"Do you know what that old cow did to me last night?"

Heather didn't want to know, but Elissa charged ahead anyway. "She, or one of her followers, sent room service to me at midnight, two and four this morning. Two meals of rare steak followed by steak and eggs for breakfast. Besides interrupting my sleep, she knows I'm vegan."

When Heather didn't comment, Elissa changed the subject. "Have you and Mr. Smiley decided if you'll look for Kira Kelly?"

"About that," said Heather. "It seems you aren't the only person who wants us to look for Ms. Kelly."

"Does that mean you'll take the case?"

"This is where things get complicated. Steve and I have a policy that we represent only one client at a time. We accepted another person's offer."

"Who?" demanded Elissa

"That's confidential," she said in an even tone.

"Have you started looking for her?"

"Everything pertaining to the case is confidential."

Violet eyes flashed. "Perhaps I should hire another investigator who isn't so... confidential."

"That's your decision. Thank you for the scarf. I'll leave you to your campaign."

12

———————

Inside the banquet room, tables bristled with baked goods worthy of a Paris *patisserie*. Fresh fruits and juices occupied a separate table. Four coffee stations lay scattered around the room. Teams of baristas stood behind cappuccino machines, ready, and more than willing, to deliver super-caffeinated delights.

Heather looked at the bounty and determined the hotel kitchen overcompensated for last night's excuse for a happy hour. She wondered if the other conferences received such elaborate fare.

The clearing of a woman's throat brought Heather's attention to Kate. After exchanging good mornings, Heather commented on Kate's scarf.

"I hope you don't think I'm taking sides," said Kate. "My neck freezes at these conventions. I'll put it away if the rooms are warm."

"I'm neutral too," said Heather. "I didn't think about packing a scarf, but I'll not hesitate to put it on if I feel a draft."

Before Kate could say anything else, Heather pivoted to a related topic. "You have a Midwest accent. I'd think you're used to chilly air blowing down your collar."

She laughed. It sounded genuine, refined, and feminine. "That was my fate as a young starving writer. I'm now a snow bird. I spend half my year with the breezes from Lake Michigan keeping me from melting, but come the first frost of fall, I fly south and allow zephyrs from the tropics to warm my weary bones. Living as a two-season nomad appeals to my internal thermostat more than frozen eyelashes or all-day summer saunas. The change of scenery also enhances creativity."

"You have a way with words," said Heather.

"Thank you." She paused and lowered her voice. "Did you and Steve look over the report from the private investigator?"

"I read it last night."

"What do you think?"

Heather shrugged. "He did a thorough job."

A look of worry crossed Kate's face. "Your praise sounds qualified. Did he miss something?"

"Don't get me wrong," said Heather. "He did everything a PI should do."

"But?"

"Steve and I have resources we call on that a normal PI doesn't have."

"That goes without saying." A hand softly squeezed Heather's forearm. "You wouldn't be speaking at this conference if you were two ordinary gum shoes. Please tell me what makes you two so successful."

"It's Steve really," said Heather. "He was the top homicide detective in Houston before being medically retired. During his tenure, he developed a network of contacts that's extensive. Some wear badges and some wear prison stripes. Steve may be blind, but he can pick up his phone and find out what he needs to know. Some top lawmen in the nation are his eyes, ears, feet and hands. If that doesn't work, he'll contact some of the more disreputable citizens and press them for information."

"That's fascinating. What do you bring to the table?"

"I'm Ivy League educated and come from a wealthy family.

My college and law school friends went for national and international careers. Many are in the State Department, but I also have close friends in the FBI, CIA and Justice Department. If I need information of a national or international nature, I can usually obtain it."

Kate's eyes brightened. "I have to be the most blessed writer in the world. You're the personification of the heroine in a new mystery series I'm developing. My protagonist will be a wealthy, strong-willed female who uses her family fortune and college contacts to solve murders that have everyone stumped. I'll put her in exotic locations with a hint of romance." Kate's eyes widened with excitement as her words tumbled out. "She'll have a ditsy sidekick that hinders as much as helps and a pet of some sort that she takes everywhere. Perhaps I'll give her a parrot and put her on a private yacht that she sails into trouble."

"What about a blind partner?" asked Heather.

"That wouldn't work. My readers expect a single female protagonist and a dull-witted partner. One of the cardinal rules of writing is to give the readers what they want. A second hero doesn't work for my genre."

Harsh sounds emanated from across the room. Heather cast her gaze toward the trad tribe. "It looks like the ladies-in-waiting for the court of Queen Hazel are encouraging the removal of scarves from their wayward disciples."

They watched as women stripped the scarves from their necks and stuffed them into book bags or purses.

Kate shook her head. "Why?"

Heather leaned in and spoke in confidence. "Elissa trademarked WMWA and had it printed on the scarves. She worked a sub-let deal with a vendor and Hazel can't shut down her booth."

"Oh, dear," said Kate, followed by a sigh that combined exasperation with lament. "I underestimated Elissa. I didn't realize WMWA wasn't trademarked. Let's try to calm Hazel. She's not well, and I'd hate to see her on the floor."

"Too late. Hazel's feet didn't get under her fast enough in the hallway. No serious harm, but I bet she picked up a bruise or two."

Alarm crossed Kate's face. "She should have given up last year."

Both women shoved their scarves into Heather's leather brief case. The trip across the room didn't go unnoticed by Hazel. She stood erect, as if confronting intruders.

"Well?" challenged Hazel. "Have you two come to finish me off?"

"Good morning, Hazel," said Kate. "Heather has some questions for you. Do you have a few minutes you could spare? I promise it won't take long."

"Please?" said Heather as she followed suit and groveled.

Hazel huffed. "If it will keep me from being accused of not being gracious, I'll give you three minutes."

Hazel winced as she sat, but soon replaced the pained expression with pursed lips and an unfriendly stare. An arthritic finger pointed. "I saw you two hide the scarves. You only did that to appease me, which means you must want something."

Kate looked at Heather and gave a quick nod.

"Kate and I are neutral parties. We apologize if the scarf offends you. It's not intended to telegraph that we wanted to wear the uniform of the indies. To me, it's a pretty scarf and a nice souvenir. Nothing more."

Kate placed a hand over Hazel's gnarled fingers. "Do you believe Elissa is giving those scarves away as a personal attack on you?"

"What else could it be?"

"Perhaps she's seeking inclusion."

Hazel bristled. "Pish-posh! I've heard that mantra for years. They're intent on degrading and destroying the writing industry."

Kate changed her tactic. She leaned back and spoke in a matter-of-fact tone. "Years ago, you were just like Elissa."

Hazel issued a loud, "Humph."

"It's true. Authors had no way to hone their craft other than sit in boring college classes. You aligned yourself with a handful of brave authors older than yourself and set out to form an organization that would help aspiring mystery writers develop their skills. Then your band of sisters taught them how to navigate the waters of publishing. You used the latest technology of the time and broke away from conventional thinking. You were a true revolutionary."

"It was different back then."

"Yes. And it's different now."

Hazel sat silent for long seconds. The skin on her face sagged, as did her shoulders. "I know change is upon us, but it's coming too fast. There's so much to lose." She cast her gaze across the room. "It's their arrogance that puts my teeth on edge."

Heather saw it coming. Hazel threw back her shoulders, sharpened her gaze and lifted her drooping chin.

"I know what I'll do," said Hazel with steel in her voice. "We'll fight fire with fire. If the indies want to raise a blue battle flag, then we'll raise a red one." She looked at Kate. "How long will it take to have red scarves printed up?"

"I'm not sure."

It was one of those times that Heather's words outpaced her brain. "You'd have better luck with t-shirts."

For the first time since they sat down, Hazel smiled. "Excellent suggestion, Ms. McBlythe. I'll dress my ladies in blazing red and Lara Lovejoy will march to victory as our new president. Change may come, but we will temper it with time."

Kate looked away, but Heather could see the author's eyes rolling back. She returned her gaze and smiled at Hazel. "Speaking of Lara, I haven't seen her this morning."

Hazel looked around with worry creasing her forehead. "Nor have I."

"That reminds me," said Heather. "Why did she send the report to me last night by courier?"

Hazel ignored the question. A snap of her fingers brought two lieutenants sailing in at flank speed. "If you'll excuse me, I need to find her." She ended the conversation by extending a hand to Heather. "Thank you for suggesting the shirts. I'm glad to hear you haven't gone over to the indies."

Heather and Kate returned to neutral territory with Kate issuing a sigh. "That didn't turn out like I'd hoped, but it's good to see her with the old fire burning again."

Heather considered the word fire. A flame can benefit or destroy. What would Hazel and Elissa's fires do? She wasn't prepared for Kate's next announcement.

"I'm off to meet Steve. He said it's something important and there's talk of a murder last night in the hotel."

Heather nodded. "Unfortunately, we're already involved."

Kate's eyes widened. "How interesting." She leaned toward Heather and whispered, "Don't worry. I know how to keep a secret. I'd hate for this mob to catch wind that a genuine murder case is being investigated by two of our speakers. They'd stick to you like gum on a cat and you'd get nothing accomplished."

13

Kate met Steve as he stepped off the elevator. She took his hand and placed it on her shoulder. "There's a rumor going around the convention about a murder last night. I found a quiet place where we can talk."

He confirmed the homicide and told her his knowledge of the details amounted to place and approximate time. "Let's go to the front desk and have them direct us to Hotel Security."

The acoustics changed as the red-tipped cane tapped down a hallway with the floor made of vinyl composition tile over concrete. "Tell me what you see."

"We're in the bowels of the beast and it looks like any other utilitarian office building, with steel-framed heavy doors with plastic placards showing the room's function. The first office we passed belonged to the manager, bookkeeping came next, followed by personnel." She came to a stop. "Here we are, the hallway stops at Hotel Security."

Once inside, they took three steps before being stopped by a voice that sounded like a rock crusher. "If you're the people that need to see the security tapes of the garage, you're out of luck."

Steve stuck out his hand. "Steve Smiley. Are you the director of hotel security?"

"Right. Captain Malone's the name."

The grip from a meaty paw came and went with undue speed. "You sound like you might be from the same neighborhood the victim came from," said Steve.

"Could be, but that Calano kid would'a been in diapers when I moved to Miami."

"You didn't know him or his family?"

"Hey, what's with all the questions?"

The response reminded Steve of the hundreds of interviews he'd conducted with tough street kids who'd answer a question with one of their own. He dispelled the tension with an inappropriately boisterous laugh. "It's an old habit I picked up when I was a cop. What about you? Where did you first carry a badge?"

"Look, Mr. Smiley. You came here to look at the tapes from the underground garage. There aren't any because the cameras down there don't work."

The door to the hallway opened and Steve lifted his chin. "Detective Warner, glad you could join us. I'd like you to meet Captain Malone, the chief of hotel security."

The room grew quiet until Malone shuffled his feet. "Sorry I couldn't help you. I need to make my rounds."

Steve held up a hand. "Before you leave, do you mind if we look at your surveillance equipment?"

"Help yourself. Right through that door."

The door to the hallway closed with more force than necessary. Quick steps faded down the hall.

"He wasn't much help," said Kate.

Steve didn't reply. Malone had revealed more than Kate realized.

"By the way," said Kate. "How did you know it was Detective Warner when he came in?"

"Yeah," said Warner. "How could you tell?"

Steve tapped the side of his nose. "You walk with a heavy footfall and use a distinct body wash. I noticed it when you and Detective Vance came to visit this morning. I surmised Vance takes morning showers while you shower before you go to bed. Both you and Vance must have received a call to come to the hotel sometime between midnight and three. You still smelled fresh while Vance reminded me of my dirty clothes hamper."

"Fragrances," said Kate. "I must remember to weave more of those into my descriptions."

"Is this Malone's office?" asked Steve.

"His name plate is on the desk."

"Get your phone and take a picture of everything in the room from all angles. Send them to Detective Warner and Heather."

As she scurried around the room, Kate blurted out, "You must think Mr. Malone is a suspect."

Steve placed both hands on the top of his cane. "The only thing I know is that real cops make him nervous."

"But he used to be a captain, didn't he?"

Instead of answering, Steve turned to his right. "Detective, tell Kate where you went through training and what you did your first year on the force."

"I started with Miami P.D. seven years ago, after I didn't get picked up in the draft. Like everyone else, I spent my first six months out of the Academy working with a trainer."

Steve didn't him let go on. "A real cop doesn't evade the question like Malone did. The reason he changed the subject is that he's never carried a badge."

"I'll check him out," said Detective Warner.

"We will, too," said Steve. "Are you averse to comparing notes?"

"Why don't we sit down?" said Warner in a soft baritone voice. Once settled, he said, "While Detective Vance enjoyed the company of our boss in a closed-door counseling session, I got online and did a little research on you, Mr. Smiley."

"Before you bore Kate with ancient history, what happened to Vance?"

"A three-day paid vacation. No disciplinary."

"Good."

Kate's fragrance became more pronounced as she took up her post in a chair next to Steve. "This is wonderful. I get to hear what you found out about this famous detective."

Detective Warner chuckled. "Let me put it like this. I skipped the people who wouldn't tell me anything and went straight to Steve's former partner."

A wide smile came to Steve. "How is Leo?"

"He gives his regards and said he's written you out of his will for not coming to see him. He also said you're a legend and if I have half a brain, I'll climb in your back pocket and see how a master solves a murder."

"It might be a little tight in my back pocket, but any time you want to tag along, you're welcome."

Warner issued a sigh. "That could be a problem. Detective Vance wants me to report to him every evening so he can review what I've learned, and then he'll give me instructions on how to proceed."

"Hmm. You may have to do a work-around."

"Wait," said Kate. "What's a work-around?"

Steve leaned her way. "It means you do what you have to do to get a job done, even if you fudge a little." He raised an open palm. "I'm not talking about doing anything illegal. It's more like Detective Warner forgetting to tell Vance all the details so he doesn't draw the wrong conclusion and make another mistake like he made this morning."

"He can be impetuous," said Warner. "Lately, it's been ready, shoot, then aim."

Steve massaged his chin. "What's eating at him?"

"There's talk of a forced medical retirement if his leg doesn't heal."

"I thought so." Giving no warning, Steve rose. "There's no use in all of us going to look at the video surveillance room. Catch up with me at lunch, Detective. It'll be my treat. In the meantime, we'll be at the writer's conference trying to bring peace to a rowdy group of authors."

The door closed and Steve counted twenty-two steps before he came to a stop and whispered, "Is the door to the manager's office open?"

In an equally hushed voice, Kate replied, "It's ajar, but not open to where I can see in."

Steve took six more steps, turned to his right and gave the door a push. "Mr. LaPage?"

"No, Mr. Smiley. It's Mr. Cruz, the assistant manager. How can I help you?"

Steve took a couple steps forward. "Ms. McBlythe and I are investigating a missing persons case." Steve lifted his hand toward Kate. "Ms. Bridges is helping me find my way around this morning so I can have groundwork done for Ms. McBlythe. Do you have a map of the hotel? Something that shows the basement and the food service areas?"

The chair squeaked and Steve heard the mechanical sound of a metal drawer opening. "There are two floors below street level. The basement is divided into two sections. The first is for deliveries and storage and the second is an underground garage. The next level up is maintenance, housekeeping offices, and the kitchens. New kitchen workers kept getting lost in the warren of hallways on that floor, so we developed maps to give them. Here are two copies."

"Perfect," said Steve. He turned to leave, but pulled up when Mr. Cruz said, "I hope Ms. McBlythe doesn't think the unfortunate event early this morning is a regular occurrence."

Steve spun back around. "Ms. McBlythe is prone to get a little testy when the body of an employee shows up in her hotel's parking lot."

The swallow didn't escape Steve's sensitive hearing.

Once in the lobby, Kate said, "You had that poor man sweating so much he'll need to force liquids the rest of the day."

When he didn't reply, she asked, "Are you ready to go back to the conference?"

Steve stopped. "Conference? We're going to the kitchens and then to the basement." He took one step and came to a halt. "When we get to the kitchens, you'll pretend to be Heather."

Her muscles tightened under his hand. "What?"

"Don't worry. I'll do all the talking. Heather's tied up teaching a class so I'll do my own work-around. It's important we gather information as fast as we can. Time isn't your friend in a homicide investigation."

14

"Elevator or stairs?" asked Kate.

"Stairs," said Steve, and then mumbled, "Any place there's no Christmas music."

A piece of paper rustled. "We don't have too long of a walk. The map shows the door to the stairway leading to the kitchens is through the lobby, but before we get to the shops."

As they walked, Steve considered who he wanted to speak to and determined Chef Miguel would be the right person to start with. "Does that map show you the location of the executive chef's office?"

"It's not that detailed. I'll ask when we arrive at one of the kitchens."

Kate slowed the pace. "Is my pretending to be Heather legal?"

"That's the wrong question. You should ask if it's ethical for us to lead people to believe you're Heather to obtain useful information. Intentional deceptions are murky waters and something I've struggled with for years. Keep in mind we're investigating the worst moral and legal offense there is, the intentional taking of a life by another person. We won't lie, but we can't help it if people reach wrong conclusions because they didn't ask the right questions. If this bothers you, we can go back to the writer's conference and Heather and I can begin our work later."

Kate stopped. "I've been writing about the internal moral struggles of my characters for as long as I can remember. I thought I was inside their heads and could feel their angst when they had to make a choice that rubbed against their moral fiber. They made their choices in ways that now seem cavalier. This is different, it's deeper. It's real. We'll talk to people who may have killed a man. They might kill again. I say we bend, but don't break the rules. Is that good enough for you?"

"You'd have made a good cop. Let's find Chef Miguel."

After descending a flight of stairs, the sounds of clanging, scraping and raised voices echoed in the hall.

"We're at the first kitchen," said Kate. "There's a window in the door. It's what you'd expect of a commercial kitchen. I see a steam pot, convection oven, a fry station, a walk-in cooler, and commercial ovens with gas cooktops. Everything's stainless steel and several cooks are moving around their stations. They remind me of a Rolex watch with its back off. Everything works in harmony and synchronization."

The sound of something metal crashing to the floor reached Steve's ears. Expletives and expressions of condemnation exploded with more volume than the crash.

"Uh-oh," said Kate. "There's a rack of lamb on the floor and a chef has a bug-eyed girl backed against a prep table."

Steve nudged her shoulder. "It sounds like they could use a distraction before we have another homicide. Let's go in."

The string of epitaphs sounded loud in the hall, but the volume didn't compare to what bounced off the tile floor and stainless steel. After taking three steps, Steve squeezed Kate's shoulder and took away his hand. "Can anyone tell me where I can find Chef Miguel?"

Except for bubbling in pots and the crackle of things being fried, the room fell silent as a crypt. The calm didn't last long.

"Who are you?" The voice belonged to the man with the salty vocabulary.

"I'm Heather McBlythe's partner in our private investigations firm." Steve made a slight gesture with his hand in the general direction of Kate. "McBlythe Enterprises is the principal shareholder of this hotel and Ms. McBlythe is a member of the board of directors. We need to speak with Chef Miguel."

The room reached an additional level of quietness.

"I'm Chef Miguel. Come to my office."

Muffled voices followed the trio to an office beyond a door that made a whooshing sound after Steve and Kate passed through it. Steve whispered, "Try to remember everything you see."

Shoes squeaked their way around what Steve assumed to be a desk. A chair creaked loudly.

"Please have a seat. How can I help you?"

Steve began. "We have a few questions for you that have to do with the death of Robby Calano."

Before Steve could ask his first question Chef Miguel stated, "I know nothing of it. I was home with my wife and children."

"Thank, you," said Steve. "That's one less question I must ask, but that wasn't my first question. How long have you been the executive chef here?"

"Two years, four months and five days."

"That's very exact. I've found that dissatisfied people keep track of days like that. What about you?"

The sound of a swallow told Steve the chef had taken a drink of something, most likely water since there wasn't any other smell.

"I'm not like most people," said the chef. "Working in this hotel as the executive chef is a rare opportunity. I have no one to tell me what I can and can't prepare for my special customers."

Steve opened his mouth to speak, but Kate beat him to the next question. "What about your administrative duties?"

"Everything runs smoothly. When Mr. LaPage hired me, the

management system didn't need changing. It's run like the military and I'm the top general. Other chefs take care of their areas of responsibility, and so it goes down the line until you get to the lowest paid."

"Who orders supplies?" asked Steve.

"I order mine for my specialty kitchen and the other chefs take care of their own areas. The chef in charge of breads makes her order, the salad chef makes his, and so on."

Steve shifted in his chair. "Who does the actual ordering for all the chefs?"

"That would be Ms. Evie Brooks. Her office is in the kitchen nearest cold storage."

Paper crinkled where Kate sat. "Could you show me on this map?"

"Are your orders ever short?" asked Steve.

"Not mine."

The answer left room for improvement. "What do you mean by not yours? Do the other chefs report shortages?"

"I should clarify," said Chef Miguel. "Everyone, including me, has trouble receiving all we request. This is expected because we deal with so many perishable and seasonal items."

Steve acknowledged the chef with a nod of his head. "Are you saying you and the other chefs have the same amount of shortages?"

His voice caught. "I don't go over their orders before they go to Ms. Brooks. Everyone complains about shortages, some more than others. I follow the procedures and have no trouble in receiving full, or almost full, orders."

Steve stood. "One more question, chef. Do you experience much stealing from the kitchens?"

The chef groaned a little as he rose. "I know what you're asking, and the answer is no. We work our people hard and give them a meal at no charge during their shift. We make the zero-tolerance policy on stealing clear when they're hired, and it's strictly enforced."

"By whom?" asked Kate.

"Hotel security," said the chef. "Look around the kitchens and in the hallways. I've never seen so many cameras."

Steve made a mental note to have Heather check on how many cameras were in the kitchens and how many were operational. He unfurled his cane and Kate placed his hand on her shoulder. "Thanks, Chef Miguel."

Back in the hallway outside the kitchen, the familiar voice of Detective Warner greeted Steve, who responded by saying, "I'm glad you showed up. We're on our way to talk to one more employee and then you can take us to the crime scene."

15

The distance from the first kitchen where Chef Miguel cooked his masterpieces and the last kitchen down the hallway proved to be longer than Steve expected. On the way, the heady smell of baked goods sent his taste buds into spasms of desire. Over the years he'd become a connoisseur of breads, rolls and pastries. So much so he had to limit his intake to eating out and special occasions.

"Here we are," said Kate. "Someone painted over the window."

"I'll go in first," said Detective Warner. "Sometimes a badge cuts through a lot of questions."

The hinges barely squeaked as the door to the hallway opened. Except for cilantro, chives and onions, Steve couldn't identify any of the smells coming from this kitchen. Kate stated what Steve had already suspected. "We're in the kitchen that preps salads. No ovens, but massive walk-in coolers."

Hushed voices came from some distance away, too far for Steve to make out the exact words. Kate explained, "Detective Warner is talking to a chef. He's pointing to an office on the far side of the coolers."

"We may be out of luck," said Warner as he returned. "Ms.

Brooks isn't here. The woman I spoke to said she usually arrives anywhere between 11:00 a.m. and 1:00 p.m."

"That seems a little late to be starting a workday," said Kate. "But I've never researched the operations of food service in a large hotel and conference center such as this. It may be perfectly normal."

"Or not," said Steve. "Who knows, it might be something you could work into a future novel."

Kate's mellow laugh bubbled out. "Steve, you're beginning to think like a writer. We look for inspiration and ideas in the most unusual places. A hotel kitchen might be worth exploring, especially for a murder mystery. Think about the knives, cleavers, boiling liquids and freezers and..." She laughed again. "My imagination breaks free and my words can't help but run after them."

"Let's look at Ms. Brooks' office," said Steve.

"She's not there," said Kate.

"That's all right. Describe what you see. You can learn a lot about people by observing their office. The same goes for someone's home. People will tell you what's important to them by how they decorate. Most family-oriented people have photos of their spouse or kids. Sales people like to show their awards. People who count themselves as professionals display diplomas while politicians have photos of themselves shaking hands with dignitaries. Things get interesting when you find unusual things."

"Like what?" asked Kate.

"It could be anything," said Steve. "I worked a case once where an elderly gentleman had an unopened can of Schlitz beer on his mantle. It looked like a simple home invasion, but turned out to be the murder of the man's wife. The old can of beer above the fireplace bothered me. I went back in the man's past and discovered an accident in high school that killed his prom date. The official reports didn't mention that he'd been drinking, but I tracked down two classmates who confirmed he'd downed nine beers that night."

"Are you saying he killed his wife?" asked Kate.

"He never got over his first love or the guilt that haunted him. He took out a big insurance policy on his wife and hired a hit man. The hired killer got greedy and stole things other than what the old man told him he could take. A rifle covered by insurance showed up at a pawnshop. The hit man broke down in questioning and told us who hired him."

"I see," said Kate. "Something as simple as an out-of-place can of beer turned out to be the string you pulled to unravel the case. That's impressive."

"Here we are," said Detective Warner. "There's not much to see because the blinds to the windows are closed and there's a piece of black paper in the window in the door."

Kate added, "There's a box for correspondence and another one labeled REQUISITIONS hanging on the wall by the door."

"Anything else?" asked Steve.

"Not a thing," said Detective Warner.

Steve scratched his chin. "Kate, this is the difference between a real investigation and fiction. We spend a lot of time chasing down people who aren't where you think they should be and knocking on doors when nobody's home. That doesn't mean this was a waste of time. We now know some things about Evie Brooks. She keeps irregular hours and doesn't like people looking in her office."

He turned to the direction they came. "Let's get down to the garage where they found Robby."

"THERE'S NO POLICE TAPE," SAID KATE.

"You sound disappointed." Steve's words bounced off the hard surfaces. The smell of exhaust fumes, tires and concrete mingled to give the place that unique garage smell.

"I expected at least a chalk outline of the body on the concrete."

Detective Warner chuckled. "That's more legend than fact.

This crime scene was thoroughly processed and then cleaned. The manager threw a fit to get it done so the high rollers staying at the hotel wouldn't be inconvenienced. We had to block off access to this part of the basement until the team wearing white suits and blue booties finished."

"Describe the garage for me, Detective," said Steve.

Detective Warner cleared his throat. "You're aware that if Detective Vance finds out I brought you here and discussed the case with you, he'll chew a couple inches off my backside."

Steve waited, saying nothing.

The young detective sighed. "I guess this is all part of the work-around you told me about. We're in the VIP garage. The high-rollers like you and Ms. McBlythe who occupy rooms that would cost me two weeks salary have access to it and a special elevator. A few of the top management in the hotel park here alongside the Mercedes, Bentleys and limos. It can also accommodate two or three luxury buses, mainly for touring celebrities. It's separated from the hotel's delivery docks by a chain-link fence that runs up to the ceiling."

Steve nodded. "This is a strange place to kill Robby. What was he doing here?" Steve wagged his head. "Tell me about the wounds."

"Two shots. One entered the back and clipped the liver. The second was also a through-and-through, but it caught him in the pump and blew out the aorta. It must have just grazed the ribs coming and going."

"Did you find casings or the rounds?"

"Neither."

"Did the second shot enter the chest or the back?"

"Chest."

Steve formed his right hand into a pistol and pointed it at Kate. "Turn around." He heard her feet shuffle. "Bang. The first shot caught him either when he wasn't looking or he was running away. It either spun him around or stunned him, and he turned to face his assailant."

He asked Kate to turn around. "Bang. The second shot is the kill shot. Robby drops and it's all over for him. Did you find splatter?"

Kate let out a soft moan.

"No," said the detective.

"Powder residue on the clothes?"

"Trace elements, but no burns. It wasn't up close."

"Any idea of the caliber?"

"We're waiting on a full autopsy, but you know it'll be a guess unless we can find the slug or a casing."

"Give me your best guess as to caliber."

"Don't hold me to it, but nine mils and forty calibers are popular these days."

"How much blood at this site?"

"Not enough."

Steve nodded. "That means the murder took place somewhere else, and they dumped him here. Was there any blood on the stairway or in the VIP elevator?"

"None. We also checked the loading dock next door and the service elevator that's used mainly for food deliveries. We found all kinds of blood, but I'm not betting on any of it being human. They carry a variety of meats upstairs on that elevator, and it doesn't look like they're too particular in cleaning it. We might get lucky and find a match to the victim, but I'm betting all we find is beef and pork blood."

"Or lamb, or venison, or chicken, or goose, or duck, or shark, or tuna, or who knows what they cook in this place," said Steve.

Steve ran through as many possibilities as he could to explain how and why Robby came to be dumped in the VIP underground parking lot. He came up with only two viable answers from the information he had. "The murder occurred somewhere other than the hotel and they brought him back here; or, it took place in the hotel and someone wants to make it look like it happened in the garage."

"Vance thinks it happened away from the hotel by someone

who knew him," said Warner. "He's going behind the captain's back and asking other detectives to check out what happened to Calano when he went home to get clothes and a toothbrush. I'm supposed to concentrate on the chefs and cooks. If you need me, I'll be in the kitchens trying to find out who disliked Robby enough to want him dead."

Something told Steve he needed to dig deeper. Later that night, he and Heather would come back and discover where the murder took place.

"Kate," said Steve. "We need to get back to the convention. Let's see how the Hatfields and McCoys are getting along."

BACK ON THE MAIN FLOOR, KATE STOPPED TO SPEAK TO A woman with a voice that sounded like a distressed parakeet. Steve knew the way to the writers' conference, so he dropped his hand from Kate's shoulder and continued on to give her privacy. What he hadn't counted on were changes made during the night and the obstacles now standing in his way. Sixteen steps after entering the hallway leading to his destination, the tip of his cane failed to warn him and he walked into something prickly. He extricated himself from whatever it was with no damage.

"Hold on, Steve, I'll help you."

"What's going on, Kate? This hall was empty last night."

Slim fingers directed his hand to rest on her forearm.

Steve pointed at the thing he'd run into. "What's that blocking the hall?"

Kate's voice held a hint of mystery in it. "A Christmas tree appeared in the night. Santa must have deployed a company of elves to decorate the hallways and lobby." She paused. "I'm sure you noticed the music is louder than last night. Period-dressed carolers will make their rounds this afternoon."

Steve groaned.

"What's the matter? No Christmas spirit?"

"Ba-humbug."

A laugh pealed out that reminded him of a mid-sized silver bell in a bell choir. He took in yet another waft of her distinct perfume. Subtle, expensive and unforgettable.

"If there are no more obstacles, I should be able to find my way," said Steve.

Her free hand covered his. She gave it three soft pats. "The elves felled a forest and festooned the trees with all things bright and shiny. I'm afraid you must put up with me a while longer as we navigate a trail through these enchanted woods."

"It seems I'm still in need of a seeing-eye author. Lead on."

Steve tried to memorize the winding route, but light conversation broke his concentration. He resigned himself to enjoy the trip. Without warning, his thoughts turned to Maggie, his deceased wife. She, too, could rattle on about the most mundane things, but he never tired of hearing her voice. What would he give to spend another Christmas with her? His pace slowed to that of a fatigued toddler's pull-toy.

"Are you all right?"

"Huh?"

The voice came again, coated with concern. "What is it, Steve? Is something wrong?"

He took in a big breath. The reason he didn't like Christmas caved in on him. Everywhere he turned he could hear, smell, and touch things that brought Maggie's face into full view. Blindness had locked the visage of a vibrant, spunky blonde in his mind. She didn't age or change; always the imperfect, perfect Maggie. She loved Christmas more than any other holiday and took him along for a ride that ended much too soon.

A spine-shiver brought life back in focus. "Kira Kelly," said Steve.

"You changed gears fast. My mind's still wrapped around the murder of the chef and why someone would place his body in the parking garage."

Steve flipped his hand. "I had to work on multiple cases. I

guess I got used to switching one off and turning the other on. I was thinking about what questions I'll ask the PIs when they return my calls."

He told a lie, but a lie of self-defense. He hadn't been thinking about Kira, but he needed to. *Concentrate on Kira's disappearance. Focus on Robby Calano.* He couldn't revisit the mental rabbit hole of a make-believe Christmas with Maggie if he wanted to maintain his sanity.

After pretending to dig sleep out of his eyes and replacing his sunglasses, Steve turned an ear to the direction of voices. "I don't hear gunshots or screams. Elissa and Hazel must be in neutral corners."

"More likely they're reloading." Kate's voice brightened. "There's a coffee service and a selection of yummy pastries down the hallway. Why don't we blow our diets?"

"If they have cranberry scones, I may skip the conference."

16

———

Heather cruised the room, catching snatches of conversations sprinkled with laughter and dipped in anticipation. For a few moments, she thought the conference might proceed without the verbal jousting she'd witnessed since leaving Houston.

A stirring came from the side of the room occupied by the tribe of die-hard traditional writers. Women's hands cupped over the ears of other women, the telltale sign of a rumor spreading.

Messengers scurried to Hazel's throne and delivered the latest report. With each one, the corners of Hazel's mouth turned further and further downward. She pulled herself up with the help of a loyal subject and then slapped the helping hand away once she'd become vertical.

The tip of Hazel's cane popped against the hardwood dance floor like a loud tap from a dance shoe with each step she took. Her gaze locked on the door leading to the hallway. The room fell silent. A path cleared as people shuffled backward.

"Here we go again," mumbled Heather to herself. "I'd better beat her to the hallway. She looks like she's out for blood and I bet it's Elissa's."

The parted sea of women flowed together after Hazel passed.

Wide-eyed and transfixed, they formed a formidable barrier. Heather had to weave her way through them, exclaiming, "Excuse me, pardon me," as she went. She somehow made it to the door in Hazel's wake.

Elissa looked up from passing out scarves to new arrivals.

Steve and Kate approached out of the forest of decorated trees. Heather intercepted them before they stumbled onto the battlefield and leaned in close enough so both could hear words meant for only them. "Hold on to your hats. Something set Hazel off."

Steve spoke in a similar hushed tone. "Get us closer."

"If you'll excuse me," said Kate. "I need to run to my room."

Heather wondered if Kate wanted to avoid being drawn into a battle. Hazel's blustery arrival removed all passing thoughts.

"Ms. Lutz!" shouted Hazel as she limped to within six feet of Elissa. "I want answers and I want them now."

Elissa threw back her shoulders and took two steps forward. "I'm right here, Mrs. Smallgrass. There's no need to raise your voice."

The two women faced each other from an uncomfortably close distance. The height difference went to Elissa by a good eight inches. Hazel did her best to stand as erect as possible. "What have you done with her?" Her words and fiery anger made her seem taller.

Elissa moved several steps away and returned to straightening a stack of scarves. Over her shoulder she said, "I have no idea what you're talking about. Have you come for a scarf?"

Hazel slammed the tip of the cane into the carpet. It made only a slight thud, which seemed to incense her all the more. She took a step forward and raised the tip of the cane, giving her the appearance of a teacher using a pointer. "You know perfectly well what I'm talking about. Lara Lovejoy is missing. What have you done with her?"

Elissa turned to face the threat and stammered. "Lara is missing? Are you sure?"

"Don't play innocent. You've made it perfectly clear that you and your henchmen will stop at nothing to wrestle control away from us." She raised her chin even higher. "I warn you, Ms. Lutz, I'll not hesitate to involve the authorities if Lara is not immediately returned to this conference."

Tented hands on hips telegraphed that Elissa did not respond well to accusations. She took a step forward and pushed the tip of Hazel's cane to one side. "You silly old woman. You're making false accusations and strutting about like you have a divine right to say whatever wicked things come into your age-impaired mind. Go ahead. Call the police. Do you know what they'll do?" She didn't wait for an answer. "They'll listen and nod their head and write a few notes. Then you'll hear the same thing we heard when we tried to find Kira."

Elissa's voice shifted to mimic the deep voice of a male policeman. "Ma'am, since there's no sign of foul play, and this Lovejoy woman has received no threats, there's nothing we can do. You can wait seventy-two hours and file a missing person report if she doesn't show up. Most likely you'll hear from her by then."

Hazel changed the grip on her cane. Her knuckles turned white and her face took on a deep shade of red.

Heather moved to stand between the two women. Steve spoke up. "I'm afraid Ms. Lutz is right."

Both women spun to face Steve. He directed his words to Hazel. "The police won't do anything for at least seventy-two hours. But that doesn't mean Ms. McBlythe and I have to wait. We can get started looking for Lara immediately."

Heather chimed in, "The first thing we need to know is what steps have been taken to find Lara. Who was the last person to see her or speak to her?"

Elissa answered the two questions with a shrug and a blank look.

Hazel responded with a weakened voice. "She called me last night after taking dinner in her room. You already know she missed last night's mixer. The day's travel and excitement of the upcoming election drained her, so she begged off from a late-night strategy meeting."

"And this morning?" asked Steve.

"I tried calling her at six-thirty. She didn't answer. I assumed she was in the shower. I've been sending her text messages all morning, and I sent three messengers to her room. The last one returned with yet another negative report. That's when I came to confront Ms. Lutz." Her gaze shifted to Elissa as embers of anger threatened to ignite into another flame.

Heather took two steps to her left so Hazel would have to pivot to see her. She needed to get the two women to stop staring at each other.

Steve drug his hand down his face. "Heather, could you get with the hotel manager and have him let you into Lara's room?"

"I'll go now. If Lara isn't in her room and a thorough search of all restaurants and common areas turns up blank, then we need to take the next step."

"What's that?" asked Hazel.

Steve said, "I'll need you to address all the attendees and ask if anyone saw or spoke to Lara after you spoke with her last night."

Heather added. "If that doesn't pan out, I'll check the security tapes from last night until now."

Hazel nodded to show she agreed with the steps proposed. She turned a slow half-circle and took an unsteady step. Two stout women took their places on each side, ready to make sure a repeat of the earlier fall didn't take place.

Heather moved to Steve's side. "Do you want me to take you inside and get you settled? The opening session should start in fifteen minutes."

Elissa took Steve's hand and placed it on her arm. "I'll take care of Steve. You find Lara before that crazy old bat has me thrown in jail."

Steve grinned. "I'm getting passed from one good smelling

woman to the next. I could get used to this." He took a breath and held up an index finger. "One more thing, Heather. Detective Warner is in the kitchen area. Let him know about Lara."

"Do you think the cases are related?"

Steve didn't answer.

17

Feet shuffled past. Multiple fragrances of colognes, perfumes and lotions came and went. Steve also picked up on accents and dialects from different parts of the country.

"The trolly is leaving. You'd better hang on," said Elissa.

His raised hand didn't make it to her shoulder until he lifted it higher. "You're tall," he said.

"That's one thing that made me a successful model." She paused. "Five eleven. What else can you deduce about me, Mr. Detective?"

"You're wearing heels that would give most women nosebleed and you have expensive tastes in clothes. I know cashmere and silk when I feel them. My guess is that you didn't always have money. You must have grown up in a rough neighborhood. That's where you learned not to let anyone push you around. You accomplished fame and fortune faster than you thought possible, but the photo shoots grew old. So, you took your bankroll, and your cat, and moved to Houston to avoid New York's taxes."

"How did you know I have a cat?"

"I have an excellent sense of smell. Also, everything I told you I learned from my internet search on you last night."

Elissa erupted with a street-laugh, loud and rough.

The noise of hundreds of conversations sounded like the roar of a giant waterfall when they entered the conference room. Elissa led him into the room and stopped.

Steve found the front legs of the chair by tapping with his cane. His hand reached down and he made out the height and dimensions of a standard banquet-room chair with a metal frame, the back and seat padded and covered by a tightly woven rough fabric.

He folded his cane, placed it under his chair and waited. "Can we leave a seat for Heather?"

"Sure. Do you think she'll be long? We only have a few minutes until it's time to start."

"That should be plenty of time. Either Lara is in her room or she isn't."

"I'll be right back."

The thought crossed his mind that Lara might be in her room, but in no condition to come to the conference. He mentally clicked off plausible reasons. She could be sick, unable to decide what to wear, hung over, injured, or dead. He blamed the last reason on his imagination and too many years working homicide.

He put further macabre thoughts aside when Elissa returned and said, "Here's your coffee and scone. I see some ladies I need to check on. Will you be all right by yourself?"

"I'm never alone as long as I have coffee and something to eat."

A kiss landed on his forehead. "You have a delicious sense of humor, Detective Smiley."

Steve sat with his hands on his lap, mildly amused and embarrassed by the unexpected show of affection. He raised the cup to his lips, savoring the moment and the coffee.

Heather's voice broke into his thoughts. "I can't leave you alone for a moment, can I?"

"Huh?"

Heather assaulted his forehead with a napkin. "Two red lips

found their way to your forehead. By the color, I'm guessing you and Elissa have been up to something."

"She got me when I wasn't looking."

They both had a chuckle. "What did you find out?" asked Steve.

"Lara wasn't there. I don't think she ever was. No clothes, no toiletries, paper covers on all the glasses and the bed wasn't slept in or even sat on."

"Interesting," said Steve.

The crinkled voice of Hazel spoke from somewhere behind Heather. "What's interesting?"

Hazel's scent caught up with her voice, a fragrance Steve's octogenarian Aunt Doris wore. He spoke as he heard Heather turn. "Lara isn't in her room."

Heather added. "There's no evidence she ever was."

"That's impossible," said Hazel.

Heather shrugged. "The assistant manager unlocked the door for me. He called down to the desk and verified the room number. The maid said she hadn't cleaned it, but the room was like she left it the preceding day, ready for occupancy."

Concern filled Hazel's next words. She spoke to herself as much as to anyone else. "What could have happened to her?"

Sometimes the answers to why people go missing are difficult to discuss. Steve stayed silent, knowing Heather would provide an answer or two that would sound indelicate coming from him.

Heather cleared her throat. "Did Ms. Lovejoy have a special friend coming to the convention?"

"No. She's quite the recluse."

"I'm tip-toeing around a hard question. Could Ms. Lovejoy have shared a bedroom with someone last night?"

Hazel shot back, "That's an absurd, slanderous accusation."

"It wasn't an accusation," said Heather. "Only a question. The reason we follow this line of inquiry is that Mr. Smiley and I have both run into this situation in our careers. It's more common in cases of marital infidelity, but people rent hotel rooms and never stay in them for many reasons."

"Such as?"

"To establish an alibi is one," said Steve.

"I assure you, Mr. Smiley, the only intrigue in Lara's life is what she creates in her stories." Hazel took in a ragged breath. "The answer to Lara's disappearance lies elsewhere. Concentrate your efforts on that minx that's bewitched you. Remnants of her lipstick remain on your forehead.

"As for you, Ms. McBlythe, I suggest you search Ms. Lutz's room."

"Fine with me," said Elissa. "You can come along if you don't trust Ms. McBlythe." She issued a narrow-eyed stare. "Even if you search my room, I doubt it will stop you from spreading poisonous rumors like you've done all morning."

"That would only prove you have her secreted away in one of your crony's rooms," countered Hazel. A foot dragged on the carpet as she made a tactical retreat.

As soon as Heather sat beside him, Steve leaned into her. "What about hotel cameras?"

Heather whispered. "The assistant manager and I spoke with the hotel security supervisor. He has three people watching video footage."

Steve leaned back and reflected. First, Kira went missing months ago. That took out the indies' candidate for WMWA president. Now, Lara vanished without a trace. Another candidate for president is out of the picture. Was Hazel as infirm as she claimed to be? Could this be the desperate actions of a woman wanting to hang on to her only reason for living? Or was this all an elaborate scheme by a model seeking even more fame and fortune? They needed to dig deeper.

18

Heather congratulated Steve after he reported a standing-room-only attendance of over two hundred eager writers who peppered him with questions. Her crowd amounted to half the size of Steve's, but she'd expected even fewer than that. Discussing tax law ranked up there with watching paint dry for this group of creatives who'd much prefer to hear stories of unwinding clues that led to solving knotty murders. It didn't take them long to abandon questions relating to the advantages and disadvantages of S-Corps versus limited liability corporations. The last half of the session amounted to story-telling.

Wanting to check the progress made by the security team while she and Steve conducted their break-out classes, Heather made her way down the corridor of Christmas trees. She stopped at the front desk to ask directions to the room where security officers were reviewing video recordings, hoping to spot the missing Lara Lovejoy.

When the assistant manager heard what she needed, he spoke in a formal tone. "Please come this way, Ms. McBlythe. I'll take you."

On the way, she and Mr. Cruz made small talk which gave Heather an opportunity to take full inventory of the man. He stood at five-feet-seven-inches tall. Black hair slicked back from his face gave him a rather swarthy look. He wore a tailored version of the company uniform of black slacks, black sports coat and starched white shirt. Her eyes drifted to his footwear and took in a pair of tasseled loafers, polished to a high gloss.

"I see you're not wearing Allbirds like Mr. LaPage."

He grimaced. "Much too informal for me, Ms. McBlythe." His voice had a tiny remnant of an accent that she guessed was of Cuban origin.

"I've been meaning to order a pair," said Heather. "Have you tried them?"

He nodded. "They're scrumptiously comfortable."

"Are they really made of wool?"

"Wool and eucalyptus trees and sugar cane. I can't tell you how appreciative my feet are after a long shift."

"You've convinced me." She continued with the small talk. "Have you worked here long?"

"Fifteen years."

"You must have started young."

He gave a nod. "Right out of high school. Actually, before. I started as a dishwasher and then worked as a prep-cook. That's before they trained me on the front desk. Then I went into the management training program."

It was good to see a youthful man with drive and she told him so. He received the compliment with a nod. She wondered if he displayed such calm when he worked the high stress atmosphere of the hotel kitchen. Chefs have a well-earned reputation of being high strung and abusing prep cooks who don't live up to their standards.

"Here we are, Ms. McBlythe. Is there anything else you need?"

"I haven't seen the manager today. Could you tell him to come to the penthouse in thirty minutes?"

"I'm afraid that's not possible. Mr. LaPage isn't scheduled to work today."

"Not in the hotel? With multiple conventions going on, I'd expect him to be here."

Mr. Cruz maintained a calm demeanor. "Normally he would be, but his wife is having a chemotherapy treatment today. From what he's told me, the side effects are most unfortunate."

"I didn't know," said Heather. "How long has she been ill?"

"It's been off and on for the past two years. Two steps forward and three back, if you know what I mean."

"And this has left you with more and more of the responsibility. Am I right?"

"It's nothing. If the roles were reversed, I'm sure Brice would do the same for me." He paused. "Excuse me, I meant to say Mr. LaPage."

Heather stuck out her hand and received a firm grip. "You're doing a fine thing for Mr. LaPage. From now on you can call me Heather."

"If it's all the same to you, I'd prefer to reserve that pleasure for when staff is not around. After all, you're a director of this hotel and our sister hotels."

"As you wish."

"Ms. McBlythe, does this visit to security have anything to do with the empty room I checked out this morning?"

"One of the mystery writers is missing." She corrected herself. "More than likely she had to leave and failed to tell anyone."

"Is there anything I can do to help?"

"Get me a printout on Lara Lovejoy's reservations and bill since she checked in."

"Do you want me to check the restaurants and see if she charged any meals? Or the bars?"

"Excellent idea," said Heather. "Your assistance will save me time."

"I'll get right on it."

With that, Ricardo Cruz issued a curt bow and spun on the sole of his gleaming shoes.

Heather pushed open the door to the security office and faced a man with beady brown eyes. His name tag read Captain Malone, and he had the face and physique of a boxer, not quite a heavy-weight and not very successful. The leaning nose with a lumpy ridgeline bore silent witness to multiple breaks. Black lines of tattoos peeked out from under his shirtsleeve and collar, making Heather wonder the extent of the murals beneath the white shirt and navy sports coat.

"Any luck?" asked Heather.

He threw a thumb over his shoulder. "Nothing that will help. That Lovejoy woman never went in or came out of her room."

"I saw her check in," said Heather. "Where did she go after that?"

"This is where things get screwy. The cameras show her entering a restaurant after she checked in, but they don't show her ever coming out. There aren't cameras in the restaurants, except covering the cash drawers."

"How did she leave the restaurant without being caught on camera?"

He shrugged. "There's only one way I can think of. She must have slipped out through the kitchen, then made it to a stairway without being recognized. Cameras don't cover the stairways, but we get good shots of the hallways on each floor. That's how we know she didn't go to her room."

"Let me see the footage of her checking in and going to the restaurant," said Heather.

He turned and gave a terse instruction. Heather stood and looked over the shoulder of a woman as she maneuvered a computer mouse on its pad. The images left no doubt Lara went to the restaurant after she checked in.

"Run it back to where she enters." Heather hadn't noticed it before, but Lara carried a single small travel bag, the kind that could fit in an airplane's overhead compartment.

After straightening her posture, Heather summarized what she'd seen. "Lara checked into the hotel yesterday afternoon with only a carry-on bag. She went immediately to the first restaurant past the lobby and disappeared." She turned to Captain Malone. "How many exits does the restaurant have?"

He scratched his cheek. "Three, with another in the kitchen that leads to a hallway for staff to come and go so they don't mingle with the guests on the main concourse."

"That means we don't know how much time Ms. Lovejoy spent in the restaurant or which exit she used."

Captain Malone pointed at the screen. "It wouldn't be hard for her to put on a wig or hat, change her clothes and leave from any of four exits. Cameras don't cover all the exits very well, and not at all if she went through the kitchen."

"Are you saying cameras don't monitor the hallways used by the staff?"

"Some are, some aren't."

"What about the basement? Could she have gone there?"

"Possible," said Malone.

Anger rose in Heather. "The basement should be the one place with active surveillance. That's where deliveries are made and VIPs park. Some are heads of state."

Malone stiffened. "I sent memos to Mr. LaPage and hotel maintenance. He said he'd take care of it."

"That's not good enough, Mr. Malone. You're in charge of hotel security, not Mr. LaPage and not maintenance."

Heather had seen and heard enough. Her stomach growled a complaint about it being time for lunch and she still didn't know what happened to Lara. She needed to relay what she learned, and Steve needed to brief her on his morning with Kate. It occurred to her again how odd it was for him to single the writer out to go with him on a murder investigation.

She turned to leave when Malone asked, "Do you want me to call Mr. LaPage and tell him you want the security cameras in the basement fixed? I can't authorize payments to vendors without his signature."

Her first inclination was to give a positive response, but then she thought better. "No. I need to evaluate all the hotel's security measures. Don't bother Mr. LaPage."

As she passed the manager's office, she heard a heated conversation in Spanish on the other side of the door. She couldn't make out all the muffled words, but understood enough to cause her eyebrows to rise. Mr. Cruz wasn't pleased with Chef Miguel's narrow focus on his cooking at the expense of not knowing what was going on in his department. The conversation came to an abrupt and unharmonious conclusion as the door cracked open and the two men gave each other a parting shot.

Scurrying down the hall and into the lobby, Heather stood behind an ice sculpture and waited. A man that reminded her of a bear wearing a chef's uniform breezed past, wearing a deep frown and mumbling in Spanish. She looked up to see the serene countenance of Ricardo Cruz. He slicked back his hair with an open palm, straightened his tie and took up his station behind workers at the front desk. Her suspicion of the man moved up a couple of notches. He possessed more grit than met the eye, including a temper that he could turn on and off at will.

The elevator deposited Heather in the penthouse's entry as voices cascaded from the dining room. Steve greeted her before Bella or Detective Warner had a chance to. "I ordered a salad for you. Room service should be here with our lunch any time."

"Thanks," said Heather as she kicked off her heels and slipped onto a dining room chair. "Did you have a productive morning?"

For the next ten minutes Steve, Heather and Detective Warner swapped notes of their activities while Bella stood at a floor to ceiling window watching stunted waves break and surfers trying to catch the meager offerings, if only for brief rides.

"Bella," said Steve. "Come here. I have something I'd like for you to do for me."

She returned to the table where she flopped down and played with her fork. "What is it?"

"Isn't there a banquet tonight for the vendors at your fishing exposition?"

"Not a fancy banquet, more like a happy hour with a buffet. I'm not going."

"Why not?" asked Heather.

She shrugged. "I don't know. I just don't feel like it. There won't be many women, and the guys always drink too much."

Steve rested his hands on each side of his plate. "I need you and Detective Warner to attend. It's an important assignment that might lead us to who killed Robby."

Bella and the detective made eye contact. He nodded and Bella straightened her posture. "What do you need me to do?"

"Take photos of the food and taste everything that's served. Make a list and give each item a grade of lousy, average, good, or excellent."

"That doesn't sound like much of an assignment."

"That's not all," said Steve. "I want you to mingle with the servers and any chefs that show up. Detective Warner didn't have much luck getting information out of anyone he spoke to this morning. We need to try a fresh approach."

The detective spoke up. "Either the people I talked to don't know much or they're afraid to say anything. I'll be watching from a distance, but it will be up to you to get them talking about what goes on in the kitchens."

Bella leaned forward. "What do I ask them?"

Steve said, "People, men in particular, love to talk to you because you make them feel special. Be yourself and ease into the conversations. Tell them you're interested in how the kitchens run because you're thinking of incorporating a seafood cooking section into your programs."

"I won't have to lie. My producer already wants to show me cooking what I catch, even though I can't make steam without burning it."

Steve pressed on. "Listen for names of people that stand out.

Pay attention if anyone doesn't want to talk to you and record their name. I'm sure they all wear nametags."

"Are you sure this will help us find Robby's killer?"

"Am I sure? No. A detective might have to bang on a hundred doors before she finds the one person who gives her the single scrap of information that brings everything together." He paused. "There's one more thing you have to do, and it's the most important thing to remember."

"What's that?"

"Don't leave the banquet room until it's time to come back upstairs."

Detective Warner nodded. "Don't be looking for me, but I'll be watching you. We'll play like we never met. I'll follow you to the hallway afterwards and make sure you make it safely back here. Understand?"

Bella looked at Steve. "Are you sure this isn't busy work to get my mind off Robby?"

Steve cleared his throat. "You just proved you have excellent powers of perception. You saw right though my plan, but you're only half right. We need to know the quality of the food they're serving and you can get people to talk to you."

"Why aren't you and Heather doing this instead of me and Detective Warner?"

"We have our own list of things to do and not much time. The conference is over Saturday night."

19

Heather knew better than to bother Steve when he fully reclined. Ensconced in the chair, Steve didn't make a move. He'd either be deep in thought, asleep, or a combination of the two. Night and day meant virtually nothing to him, and his sleeping patterns became even more unpredictable when he had a case to work on.

At nine-thirty, he jerked the handle on the side of his chair and sat upright. Bella and Detective Warner wouldn't be back for at least another hour.

The elevator ride to the first floor began without conversation, a sure sign Steve hadn't yet emerged from a place within himself where he processed every scrap of information he'd picked up since they boarded the flight from Houston and Hazel doused Elissa with coffee. Heather tried to do the same, but the ever-growing number of odd occurrences left her dazed. Had Kira, the indie author and presidential candidate, been abducted, or warned to stay away from the convention as Elissa believed? Why hadn't they heard from the private investigators Steve called?

What about Lara? She'd never stepped foot in her room, and she wasn't a figment of everyone's imagination. Was she drugged, taken to the basement and spirited away? Did the basement garage hold secrets to Robby's murder and Lara's disappearance? Could Hazel be right and one of Elissa's cohorts had her in a hotel room? Or perhaps Lara wasn't the wallflower everyone took her for.

"You're clicking your tongue," said Steve. "Stop thinking so hard. We don't have enough data yet. Let's get to the basement and you can have a look at the cameras."

The elevator door swished open, and Steve's hand found her shoulder. Heather spoke as she took the first step onto a marble floor. "Sometimes I think you know more about what I'm thinking than I do."

The fire escape stairway lay close to the hotel's entrance. Heather pulled open the door and entered an area of concrete steps and steel rails reaching both skyward and down two flights. "Grab the rail," said Heather. "We're heading down."

After consulting the map, they descended one flight. Heather said, "This must be a secondary egress for the kitchens. There's a maze of hallways."

A thousand aromas seeped into the hallway as they passed the last kitchen and rode a freight elevator down to the basement and loading dock. The smell of oil, gasoline and rubber assaulted Heather as soon as she took a step forward.

The underbelly of the hotel was divided into two unequal areas, segregated by a chain-link fence. Limousines and luxury cars nestled in the cordoned off area to her right.

The larger side of the basement was dug deeper at the docks, but the same height next to the fence. The slope at the dock looked sufficient for box trucks to unload with a pallet jack or a small fork lift. Deliveries made at this level were transferred upstairs via a freight elevator or stored in a walk-in cooler. Once again Heather described the scene to Steve.

"Where's the security camera?" asked Steve.

"Mounted on a support pillar about thirty feet away. It's

pointed at the freight elevator." She looked at a distant pillar. "There's a second camera that monitors the loading dock."

Steve didn't need to tell her to walk to the pillars holding the cameras. When they arrived at the first, she craned her neck to look for something odd or suspicious.

"It's eight or nine feet off the ground," said Heather. "I can't see the back of it."

"Is there anything to stand on?" asked Steve.

Heather scanned the area. "Nothing here. I can come back later."

Steve huffed, "I should have thought of this before we came."

Heather moved Steve until he stood within inches of the concrete pillar. "Reach out and grab the edges."

"What are you doing?"

"I'm going to climb you like a tree. Squat down while I kick off my shoes. Stand still."

Heather placed her left foot on Steve's left thigh. Her right foot hooked on his right hip. In a fluid motion, she raised herself and dug her left foot into the top of his left shoulder and brought her right foot up to the other shoulder.

"I don't remember this as a part of our partnership agreement," said Steve after groaning with each of Heather's upward steps.

She ignored him. The back of the camera came into view. "Stand up straight and I'll be able to get a good look."

Steve grunted and came to his full height. "If I'd known we'd be doing this, I would've suggested you drop a few pounds," said Steve.

"I'll have you know I weigh the same as I did in prep school."

"They must have fed you well," said Steve with another groan.

"I don't think you have much room to talk. I noticed your belt's a little snug these days." She bent her knees. "All finished. Squat down again."

Heather reversed her climb and slipped on her shoes.

"What did you see?"

"Someone cut the video cable. It's a clean cut, but it happened some time ago. The ends are rusty."

Steve knocked any residual concrete dust from his hands. "That's interesting."

The garage-style door on the VIP side of the fence jerked upward. "Company's coming," said Steve. "Let's get back in the service elevator."

"We don't have to go that far," said Heather. "This pillar is big enough to block anyone's view."

"Tell me about the fence," said Steve.

Heather scanned it. "It's chain link and goes to the ceiling. There's a gate halfway, but there's a lock on it."

"We need to check it out before we leave."

Car doors opened and closed. Heather peeked around the corner to see who was being let off on the VIP side. She turned to Steve and whispered. "Six rather scantily clad women got out of a limo and are heading upstairs on the VIP elevator."

"Their voices are high," said Steve. "Are they speaking Spanish?"

Heather ignored the question as she took another look around the barrier. "That's just what I don't need, another problem to solve."

"Trouble?" asked Steve.

"Working girls," said Heather through gritted teeth. "Except these are really girls, not women."

Tires squeaked more and squealed as the limo turned to leave. Steve waited until the sound of the garage door closing gave way to silence. "Let's stay focused on Robby. Take me to the gate in the fence."

"No drag marks or any sign of blood. Not even a gum wrapper," said Heather as they stood before the gate secured with a padlock.

"Say Robby's name," said Steve.

"Robby Calano," said Heather in a clear voice. She didn't have long to wait.

"It's red."

A chill went down Heather's back, all the way to her feet. "Is it clearer than the spot Detective Warner took you to this morning on the other side of this fence?"

"Yeah." Steve closed his eyes and allowed his head to droop. He raised his chin and spoke in a soft, reverent voice. "Take me to the place where delivery trucks unload."

Heather led him down an incline until the tip of his cane hit a wall about four-feet high. Again, she said, "Robby Calano."

Steve took in a deep breath and let it out through pursed lips. "Bright red. Robby died here."

"There's no sign of blood on the concrete and it doesn't look like they cleaned. Are you sure?"

Steve nodded. "He died in the back of a delivery truck. Find the truck and we find the slugs."

They stood without speaking. Steve, most likely out of reverence; Heather because she stood in awe of the man she called her partner. Once again, he'd displayed what she jokingly called his super-power, associative chromesthesia. It gave Steve the ability to have the perception of color at a crime scene. He wasn't alone in this ability to see colors that most can't. Artists might see everything in shades of green when painting a landscape, even before paint met a blank canvas. A composer might see the world through a blue lens when composing or directing. For Steve, he saw red, or more exactly, shades of red when he came upon the scene of a homicide. He'd refined his ability over the years and could discern between an accident and a murder. Today, he'd been able to differentiate the location of the murder from where the killers placed the body of Robby Calano.

"Let's get upstairs and come down the elevator to the parking garage. You need to check out the camera on that side too," said Steve. "But first, let's ride the freight elevator up to the kitchens. There's something I need you to look at and describe to me."

A mixture of smells including disinfectant and a cornucopia of vegetables and meats assaulted Heather on the brief ride up. Steve held his nose.

"Where do you want to go?" asked Heather as they wasted no time in stepping out of stench and into the more pleasant aromas of breads and spices.

Steve searched in front of him with his cane. "The first kitchen we come to is where they prepare salads. The office of the woman responsible for ordering all food is in that kitchen. Kate and I were here earlier today, and she described what she could. It wasn't much. We need to look in the office."

Heather stopped outside the door and looked at Steve. "Are you trying to find a new partner?"

If it wasn't two former cops talking, Heather knew the question might offend. An unwritten rule of partners with badges is that they needle each other from time to time. Not only did this keep them on their toes, but it helped them keep their emotions in check.

"Keeping my options open," said Steve. "You and that hot-shot attorney you're dating may run off and get married over Christmas. That wouldn't be so bad, but you'd move and take Max with you. Where would that leave me?"

On the fly, he'd devised the perfect comeback and exactly what Heather deserved. Without coming out and saying it, he told her he could find another partner to help him solve murders, but he'd be bereft without her Maine Coon cat. She backed away from the verbal jousting and announced, "We're at the door to the kitchen. Where's her office?"

"Past the prep tables, on the left side of the room."

Cooks looked up from their labor, but only long enough to take in the odd couple. No one challenged their presence. Heather leaned into Steve. "You must have made an impression this morning. Everyone looks like scared rabbits."

"It's not me. The word's out that the boss's boss is in town and prowling about." Steve tipped his head to the left. "We should be close."

The sign on the door read, "Evie Brooks, Director of Procurement."

"We're in luck," said Heather. "Ms. Brooks must work late."

Steve nodded. "She wasn't here when we stopped by this morning. Make sure you get a good look at her office."

Heather's knock received a quick, "I'm busy. Put it in the box." A second knock brought better results.

"Sorry about that, please come in. I'd offer you a seat, but as you can see, there aren't any. I found if I give the chefs a chance to sit, they take up squatter's rights and rant for hours."

The trim-figured woman extended a suntanned hand and gave Heather a competent shake. The wedge hairdo made two points of thick blond locks that tried to meet under a square chin. The office appeared utilitarian in the extreme, with no photos except one lone picture of Evie at the helm of a seaworthy sail boat. Otherwise, the office might have been in an army requisitions office.

"Ms. Brooks," said Steve. "I stopped by this morning hoping to meet you."

"Yes," said Evie. "Chef Miguel told me Mr. Smiley and Ms. McBlythe came by. It's a shame she couldn't come with you tonight, I'd love to meet her."

Heather opened her mouth to correct the misunderstanding, but Steve cut her off. "Ms. McBlythe is a very busy woman."

"Then she and I have something in common. What can I do for you, Mr. Smiley?"

"I'm investigating the death of Robby Calano and have reason to believe it might have something to do with large quantities of food and beverages going missing from the hotel. I'd like for you to tell me the procedures you use for ordering and receiving supplies."

The question didn't seem to ruffle Ms. Brooks in the least. In fact, she smiled with teeth so bright they looked like white porcelain. "It's really a very simple system. The chefs drop off their orders, any time, day or night, in the box outside my door. I consolidate the requests and place the orders with various vendors. When the merchandise arrives, it's unloaded on the back dock, inventoried, and brought upstairs to be distributed to the various kitchens."

"What about the cold storage I saw downstairs?" asked Heather.

"That's for after-hour deliveries. We're not staffed to have teams on the back dock at all hours, so if a delivery is late, we'll unload the truck and place the items in cold storage until the next morning."

"Is that a common occurrence?" asked Steve.

"It doesn't happen often enough to warrant hiring another team. If I'm here, I'll round up some kitchen workers. If the delivery is past eight in the evening, someone in maintenance will draft people to unload and leave everything in the walk-in cooler."

"Thank you, Ms. Brooks." Steve turned to leave, but stopped and turned back around. "Oh, one more question. Do you experience more shortages when you receive deliveries after hours?"

She shook her head. "Not that I've noticed."

Heather looked down as Evie Brooks rounded her desk. "I've seen so many people wearing Allbirds shoes since I arrived for the conference. They must be quite the rage in Miami."

"You should get a pair," said Evie. "You'll not want to wear anything else."

Steve thanked her and reached for Heather's shoulder. Out in the hallway, away from prying eyes and listening ears, he asked, "What did you think?"

Heather shook her head, even though she knew Steve couldn't see her. "The hotel needs a thorough audit and revamping of procedures."

"That's not what I meant. What did you think of Evie Brooks?"

Heather considered the question before she spoke. "There's no chance she'll be elected Miss Congeniality. Her office had all the warmth of a jail cell, and even though it's plenty big for other chairs, she made a point of keeping it where no one could sit. The only photo in the room was of her smiling as a spray of salt water came off the port side of what looked like a fifty-foot sloop she was sailing."

Steve didn't respond, which wasn't unusual, but a little maddening all the same. As they climbed a set of stairs to the main floor level, Heather asked, "What did you think about her?"

"She doesn't smell as good as Kate."

Heather barked out a laugh. "Keep going and you'll be the one eloping over Christmas."

"No way," said Steve. "There'd be no one to take care of Max."

They came full circle when they boarded the elevator and headed for the penthouse. "What's on the agenda tomorrow?" asked Heather.

"We need to trade notes on what each of us did this morning and talk to Bella."

When they arrived, Detective Warner and Bella sat in the living room downing root beer floats. Steve made his way to the recliner and folded his cane. "You two are back early."

"Yeah," said Bella. "It was boring. I must not be much of a detective. Everyone I tried to talk to clammed up."

"That's not entirely true," said Warner. "You found out some things, especially about Chef Miguel."

Heather took a seat on the couch beside Bella. "What did you learn?"

"His name is Miguel Moreno, and he's from Chicago." She paused, "Other than that, not much."

For her efforts, Heather gave her a pat on the leg. "Good job. That'll save me time in finding his personnel record."

Steve added, "And I can do a background check on him now

that we know his name."

Detective Warner directed a head nod to Bella. "Tell them about Evie Brooks."

"Not much to tell," said Bella. "Nobody likes her and they call her Miss Sunshine. She comes and goes when she wants and never talks to anyone."

Steve gave out a grunt that showed he agreed. "We met Ms. Brooks today, and she didn't impress us as being much of a people person." He took a breath and asked, "How was the food?"

Bella extended her hand and gave it a wiggle. "Only fair. Small portions of salad with one half of a cherry tomato on top, rubber chicken, green beans out of a can, mashed potatoes... the usual banquet fare, but the hot rolls were good."

Detective Warner agreed. "I've attended my share of sports banquets. The food tasted like it came out of a high school cafeteria."

Heather growled, but didn't put words to her thoughts.

Bella turned to face her. "Don't wait up for me. Detective Warner's taking me to see some of Miami's night life."

The detective held up his palms in a sign of defense. "I told her she'd have to get your permission."

Steve took over. "That's an outstanding idea, but you're responsible for her."

Heather didn't like it, but didn't know why or how to object without rupturing a relationship. Bella would be safer with the detective than she would by herself. She choked back a complaint and said, "Don't be too late and remember, just because you look like you're twenty-one, you're not."

Both Bella and the detective stood. He added, "I have more interviews to conduct tomorrow morning so we'll both be on a soft-drink diet."

Steve took off his shoes in preparation to lean back in the recliner. "Stop by about eight in the morning, Detective. We'll trade notes."

20

The next morning, flanked by two women and leaning heavily on her cane, Hazel shuffled toward Heather and Steve. She halted a step closer than appropriate and shifted her cloudy gaze from one to the other.

"Well?" said Hazel. "Have you found Lara?"

"Not yet," said Steve.

She delivered her next question as if entitled to an immediate, satisfactory answer. "What have you discovered of value?"

"We're not at liberty to say," said Heather, using her attorney voice.

Hazel took a half-step forward. "I'll not be toyed with, Ms. McBlythe."

Heather expounded on her previous statement. "We maintain strict confidentiality with our clients. That person is the only one we keep informed."

Steve cut in. "Our contracts specify that we're not obligated to keep them informed until the case is closed. We prefer not to waste time explaining details that invariably lead to more questions."

Hazel huffed in disgust. "Am I to understand you are employed by that charlatan, Elissa?"

Steve responded again. "Like I said. We maintain strict confidentiality. That means we do not disclose who hired us or anything pertaining to our investigation. However, I will tell you we have not concluded our investigation or submitted our final report."

Hazel's face turned an unhealthy shade of red. She lifted her cane, thought better of whatever she'd planned to do with it and lowered the tip to the ground. "That tells me you've made no progress in finding Lara. My only regret is that I didn't hire you. I'd have enjoyed firing you."

Both of Hazel's attendants issued frosty stares. The one on her right said, "We all know what's going on. Elissa did something with Kira. Now Lara is missing, too." She wagged a finger. "Don't be taken in by her looks, Mr. Smiley. Elissa will do anything to take over, even if that means kidnapping or killing the two women who have a legitimate shot at being the next president."

The second woman nodded her head. "Don't worry, Hazel. We won't let her get her hands on you."

The first woman added, "If Elissa gets anywhere near Hazel, we'll take care of her no matter what."

The three traditional writers turned and made their way to the stage, where the two women had to help Hazel up the steps. They settled her in a chair and one brought her a bottle of water.

Heather placed Steve's hand on her shoulder. "Were you taken in by Elissa's good looks?"

Steve let out a chuckle. "I thought the white cane and sunglasses might be a clue that I can't see. My days of ogling pretty girls ended a long time ago."

"Let's sit in the back," said Heather. "I don't want Hazel staring a hole through us while she makes the announcements for the morning sessions."

The thick crowd, many who'd attended the classes they taught the preceding day, stopped them to ask questions or thank them. They worked their way to the back row as Elissa approached. Once again Heather couldn't help but notice the woman's style and sultry beauty.

"Do you mind if I sit by you, Mr. Smiley?"

"Hello Elissa. Make yourself comfortable. How's the campaign?"

"I'm making progress, but it's still anyone's game." She looked past Steve to Heather. "Is it true that Lara is still missing?"

"Bad news travels fast," said Steve, not knowing Elissa directed the question to Heather.

"Do you think it's related to the hotel murder?" asked Elissa. "There's a rumor going around that there may be a serial killer among us."

Heather spoke up. "Whoever started that rumor has an over-active imagination."

"Heather's right," said Steve. "There's a perfectly logical explanation for where Lara is. We just don't know what it is it yet."

"You're a sly one, Mr. Smiley. My heroine uses that answer. She's a private detective, too." She patted him on the leg. "Did the report Kate sent to you help?"

"Ah, you know about that. I'm sorry, but I can't comment on any details of the case."

Three loud raps of a gavel brought the conversation to a close. Hazel leaned on the podium and spoke in a weak voice. "Please take your seats."

Those standing moved to empty chairs as Hazel looked over the top of her reading glasses.

"Again, I want to welcome everyone attending this year's convention. I hope you found yesterday's break-out sessions useful. I, for one, found the presentations on finding an agent and the proper way to write query letters to be of tremendous benefit."

Elissa issued a moan of disgust.

Hazel flipped over a note card and continued. "In other business, I regret to inform you we've had to cancel the afternoon's question-and-answer session with Steve Smiley and Heather McBlythe. It seems we made a mistake and double booked one of the breakout rooms."

A soft roar rose from the gathering. Women shook their heads, their faces telegraphing disappointment.

Elissa looked past Steve to Heather. "What did you do to make her mad? The same thing happened to a presenter last year. He taught on the future of artificial intelligence in writing and publishing. He and Hazel had a heated discussion about changes coming to the industry. She sent him packing."

Heather reached for her phone and typed as Hazel continued.

"In other business, it's our custom to gather after the last session on Thursday to receive formal nominations for next year's president. Since Saturday is our day of highest attendance, the executive committee has put off nominations until Saturday. The election will take place at 5:00 p.m. on Saturday. I will announce the results at the awards banquet later that night."

Murmurs rose from the crowd for the second time. Elissa bristled as her posture stiffened. "That manipulating old bat. I'll put a stop to this."

Steve's grip on Elissa's wrist kept her from rising. "Don't do it. She's trying to bait you into causing a scene."

Heather leaned over Steve. "Leave it to us, Elissa. We have a plan."

Steve leaned into Heather and whispered, "We do?"

Heather understood why Hazel postponed the nominations. She had to buy time to find Lara.

"One last item of business," said Hazel as she rapped the gavel again. "As you know, our sessions end this afternoon at 5:00 p.m. You are on your own for dinner."

A delivery man entered the room, pushing a cart loaded with boxes. One of Hazel's disciples directed him to the stage and motioned him to hurry. Hazel threw her shoulders back with a look of victory about her. The underling ripped open the top box and hustled onto the stage with something bright red in her hand.

"Before any of you leave," said Hazel while looking at Elissa. "Everyone is to receive their official convention t-shirts. They're complimentary and we request you wear them proudly while at this year's convention."

Hazel held up the first shirt. Large white script letters on a fire-engine red background read: *WRITING DONE WRIGHT.* In smaller letters underneath, they emblazoned the shirts with: *WOMEN'S MYSTERY WRITERS ASS.*

Snickers morphed into laughter. The spelling errors caused the authors, who lived for precision with words, to cackle.

Heather leaned into Steve and explained.

A look of puzzlement flashed across Hazel's face. She turned the shirt to where she could read it. Even from a distance, Heather could tell Hazel's face had turned crimson as she threw the shirt to the floor and white-knuckled the sides of the podium.

Hazel's focus honed in on the section where she and Steve sat. Hazel shouted into the microphone. "Elissa! You'll pay for this!"

Elissa sprang to her feet and pointed. "LIAR!" She pushed back a wave of hair that had fallen in front of her face. "I had nothing to do with this, and I defy you to offer any proof to the contrary. Don't blame me because you forgot how to spell. Don't you think it's time to upgrade to something other than a manual typewriter? Buy a computer and get a program that checks spelling and grammar."

Squabbles broke out across the room.

"Take me up front," said Steve.

Heather guided him as his cane felt the way.

"Get me on the stage and move Hazel away from the microphone."

Heather did as he said, up to a point. She positioned him

near Hazel and whispered. "Stand here, Steve. You don't need to say anything. I've summoned the cavalry."

Ricardo Cruz strode to the stage and climbed the steps. He walked confidently to the podium and put his hand over the microphone. "Excuse me, Mrs. Smallgrass. With your permission, the hotel has an announcement to make."

Hazel's shoulders rounded over. Her breath came in quick gasps. She nodded and took a wobbly step to her right. Heather and one of Hazel's escorts rushed to help her to a chair.

Mr. Cruz stood at the microphone with head erect and spoke in clear, crisp sentences. "The hotel has learned there's been a mix-up in the rooms assigned to the breakout sessions. We understand the question-and-answer session led by Mr. Smiley and Ms. McBlythe was canceled because of a logistical problem. To help rectify this, the hotel will host an open bar happy hour in this room immediately following the last afternoon session. It's our pleasure to host the Women's Mystery Writers Association, and it's our intention to make your stay memorable for all the right reasons. Therefore, all drinks and food will be complimentary, including champagne, a carving station, boiled shrimp, stuffed crab cakes and a full salad bar."

Heather took her place in front of the microphone. "Mr. Smiley and I will be available at the happy hour to answer your questions." She turned to Hazel. "Is there anything else before we're dismissed to the breakout sessions?"

Looking like it took all her remaining strength to do so, Hazel shook her head.

The gathering rose en masse and headed for the door.

Steve spoke as soon as Heather sidled up to him.

"Nice job, partner, but how much will this cost the hotel?"

"Less than cleaning up from a riot."

21

The lure of free food and drinks brought the attendees' minds away from the squabbles over politics and botched shirts. A swarm of people, almost all of them women, poured out the doors to attend the morning break-out sessions. Steve and Heather lagged and went to join Kate. The hybrid author looked on with concern narrowing her eyes as Hazel shuffled to the door with the aid of the same two women who'd promised to protect her.

Kate drew near to Heather and Steve. "Hazel needs to rest. I hope she doesn't attend any more sessions today."

Heather studied Kate's face and stated the obvious. "You really care for her."

"Everything I know about writing and traditional publishing I owe to Hazel, and each step of my early career was under her tutelage. Her knowledge is encyclopedic. Writing for a living isn't easy, and I would have quit if it wasn't for Hazel. She gave me pats on my back when I earned them and kicks in the seat of my pants when I needed them. The one thing she never did was give up on me."

"And now?" asked Heather.

A sigh came from somewhere down deep. "Hazel doesn't

know when, or even how, to quit. If she'd given up the presidency three years ago, we'd still have her as a writer and mentor. That's where her joy comes from."

"She no longer writes?" asked Steve.

"She slowed down six years ago and has submitted nothing for publication in the last four years. She spends all her energy on this organization." Kate looked into Heather's eyes as if begging for understanding. "This may sound odd, but I pray Hazel won't do something foolish like try to hang on any longer. She promised me she wouldn't."

The room had emptied, leaving the three standing in a cavern filled with chairs. Kate looked to the open doors. "When I heard Kira had disappeared, I thought Hazel would finally ease into retirement. I didn't count on Elissa rising so fast to pose a threat to Hazel."

As if awakened from a dream, she issued a vague smile. "If you'll excuse me, I'd better get to my session."

After Kate left, Steve said, "She's an honorable woman."

Heather responded with an "Uh-huh," and considered Steve's words. Stuck between her allegiance to Hazel and the knowledge that change had to come to the organization, Kate walked a tightrope. Which side would she choose at Saturday's election?

Once in the hallway, Heather asked, "We have a full day of free time. What are we going to do?"

"Kira," said Steve. "I need to go upstairs and call the private detectives again. I also want to go over the files from both PIs that Bella recorded for me." He paused. "And what about you? How are you going to spend the next seven hours?"

Heather's voice took on a sarcastic tone. "Let me see. I have shady ladies coming into the hotel through the VIP garage, a security supervisor I need to fire, lousy food being served, wholesale stealing from the kitchens, and a guest is missing. I think I have plenty to keep me busy."

Steve yawned. "I'm hoping the PI doesn't answer. I could use a nap."

"You're hopeless," said Heather. "Let's get you to the elevator before you fall asleep and I have to carry you."

"What problem are you going to solve first?" asked Steve as they walked.

"Getting rid of my crooked security supervisor shouldn't take long and it will bring me tremendous satisfaction. After that, I want to go back to the kitchens and see if I can't convince someone to talk to me about the thefts. Those two chores should fill up my morning."

Steve raised his hand to her shoulder. "Hold off on firing Malone. I'd like to keep him close until we find out who killed Robby."

They wove their way through the forest of Christmas trees and approached the elevator. Heather looked toward the hotel's entrance in time to see Detective Warner approach.

"Sorry I'm late," he said. "Bella kept me on the dance floors until my legs felt like wet noodles." He looked at Heather. "How does she eat so much pizza and not look like a sumo wrestler?"

Steve chuckled at the question. "Detective, why don't you go with Heather this morning? She'll fill you in on everything we did yesterday."

The elevator dinged its arrival and Steve boarded. Heather teasingly wished him a good long nap and set off for the security office with the detective.

The same woman who'd monitored the security screens yesterday sat alone when they arrived. "Where's your boss?" asked Heather.

"Captain Malone left shortly after you were here yesterday. I haven't seen him today."

"And the other officers that were assisting you yesterday?"

The woman averted her gaze. "The same."

Heather grabbed a chair and moved it close. "I didn't know Mr. Malone held the rank of captain before he came here."

Downcast eyes told Heather the woman had something to hide.

"What's your name?" asked Heather.

"Latrice Ohasi."

Heather took a long look at the woman who spoke with an accent that mixed English with an African dialect.

"Do you know who I am?" asked Heather.

"Your name is Miss McBlythe, and you are someone very important."

"Did Captain Malone tell you that?"

"Please, Miss McBlythe, I can't answer any of your questions."

Heather moved her chair closer. "Did he tell you not to talk to me?"

Her round eyes pooled with tears. "I can't lose this job. My family is counting on me and there's no other work for me to do."

Heather looked the woman up and down. She noticed one shoe had a sole at least six inches thick. Sympathy for the woman combined with anger. "No one will fire you, Latrice. I won't let them. However, I need you to be perfectly honest with me. What did Captain Malone say to you?"

Latrice glanced around the room with eyes wide, as if looking for a way out. Her head dipped and her chin rested on her chest. "I'm to tell you I saw nothing suspicious on any of the screens. If anything looks wrong, I'm to tell only him."

"What about the girls in short skirts that come and go on the elevator to the underground garage? Did he tell you not to talk about that?"

Detective Warner straightened his posture and took a step forward. "You need to tell Ms. McBlythe the truth."

Her head rose and dropped a single time. "That's what I'm not to tell."

"Do you have those recordings?"

"He erases them when he arrives. He told me to forget I ever saw them."

Heather took Latrice's shaking hand. "Make me a copy of last night's recording as fast as you can." She looked up. "Detective Warner is going to the end of the hall. If Malone shows up, he'll keep him busy."

She had a crooked security manager. Of that she was sure. What she didn't know was how many other things Malone had his hands on. Was he responsible for the lousy food? Probably not, but he had to know about the thefts, and that might put him on the loading dock. Steve said he had a history of violence.

"Latrice, tell Captain Malone—"

The office door flew open and Malone entered the room. He nodded at Heather and then shifted his gaze to Detective Warner. Latrice turned back to the bank of monitors and looked like she wished she could crawl into the picture.

"Can we help you, Ms. McBlythe?"

"Ah, Captain Malone. I'm glad you're here. This is Detective Warner." Heather needed to think fast to protect Latrice. "We struck out with Ms. Ohasi. She has seen no suspicious activity on any of the monitors. Have you discovered anything new concerning Ms. Lovejoy's disappearance?"

He ran his hand down the side of his face. "Nothing definite, but I have a theory. The recording shows she brought a carry-on bag with her to the hotel and into the restaurant. I think she was up to something she didn't want anyone to know about."

Needing to get Malone out of the office so Detective Warner and Latrice could copy the video, Heather said, "You know, I have another appointment to get to, but I would love to hear your theory. Would you mind explaining while we walk?"

Malone followed Heather as she pulled open the door and stepped into the hallway.

A look of superiority crossed Malone's countenance. "People do all sorts of things at conventions. I bet this Lovejoy woman had a wig, glasses and an extra shirt or jacket in that bag. Five will get you ten she's up in a room with someone she knows."

They reached the lobby and Heather stopped. "This is so interesting."

Hoping to keep him talking, she said, "So, you think she changed into a costume of sorts."

"Yeah. She puts on the disguise, scoots out the kitchen of the restaurant and meets someone in the stairway. They go to whatever floor the other person has a room on and there she is. I've seen it a thousand times."

Heather nodded. "That's plausible." She cast a thankful gaze at Malone. "If you're right, she'll probably show up today. Thank you. It's a big relief to me to know the hotel's security is in such capable hands."

For the next ten minutes she turned on the charm and joked with a man she'd like to see wearing an orange jumpsuit.

Heather hoped her relief wasn't as evident as it felt when Detective Warner walked up.

"Nothing helpful on last night's surveillance," said Warner. He rested a hand on Malone's shoulder. "I pressed your girl hard. It looks to me like you run a tight ship. Nothing of consequence happened last night, other than a couple of drunks had to be escorted out of a bar."

As Malone walked toward his office, Heather spoke to Detective Warner in a soft voice. "Did you get it?"

"Yeah."

"Do you think she'll tell Malone?"

"I told her you have connections in the State Department that might get her mom a visa to come live with her."

Heather didn't break stride. "That's a bargain for putting Malone behind bars." Her cell phone sounded a multi-note ring tone.

Steve asked, "Have you put the ladies of the evening to flight?"

"Not yet. I've been having a chat with my security director. He's dirty as a white sheet on the floor of a cattle truck."

"I need you to get background on him from the personnel files. All you can find."

"Do you think he's the ringleader?"

"I don't think so. My gut's telling me he's paid to not see things."

"I'll get on it late tonight after Malone leaves. What's next?"

"I want Detective Warner to go back to the kitchens for more interviews," said Steve. "While you're in the personnel office tonight, see if you can find anything else of interest."

"Until then," said Heather. "I'm going to do some general snooping."

22

The manager's office door stood open as Heather approached. She slowed and walked on the balls of her feet so the heels of her shoes didn't give away her presence. Peeking into the room, she observed Brice LaPage, the hotel manager, with his chin on his chest and his hands shielding his eyes. She listened to low moans for another few seconds and knocked on the frame of the door.

Looking up, Mr. LaPage cleared his throat and stood. "Ms. McBlythe, please excuse my appearance."

Red-rimmed eyes and blotchy skin gave evidence that he'd been crying, had a sleepless night, or both. He motioned for Heather to sit but said nothing else.

"I'm sorry to interrupt you, Mr. LaPage. Might I have a few moments of your time?"

He eased into his chair and pulled the cuffs of white sleeves until they formed a uniform border on his black suit coat. He tried to speak, but couldn't.

"It's your wife, isn't it?" asked Heather. She reached to his desk and retrieved the photo of a woman standing on the bow rail of a sailboat with spray jetting out to starboard and port. The picture captured the woman as she turned from facing forward. A floppy hat, sunglasses and flowing blond hair obscured her face, but that didn't matter as the photo accentuated the woman's shapely legs.

He appeared surprised, but only for a second or two. Then he nodded. "Hospice will help care for her until…" He couldn't finish the sentence.

"How long has she been ill?"

"I've lost count. It seems like forever."

"Is there anything I can do?" Heather knew the answer before she asked. It was one of those questions people throw out when they don't know what else to say.

He choked out, "It's an inoperable brain tumor. The doctors say it's a matter of weeks or perhaps only days."

Heather leaned forward. "You should be at home with her."

"I won't stay here long." He glanced around his office. "I should also tell you I haven't devoted myself to the hotel like I should. If it weren't for my staff, I don't know what I'd do."

"It takes a team," said Heather. "When one person needs help, others rise to the occasion." She sharpened her gaze. "From what I've observed, your assistant manager is most capable."

Mr. LaPage pulled a tissue from a box on his desk and dabbed the corners of his eyes. "He's been a true godsend."

Talking seemed to get Brice's mind in a better place as his voice strengthened. "I have a confession, Ms. McBlythe. Ricardo has been the true manager for the past several months. Evelyn spent most of her time at a cancer center in Houston, and I've been away from my duties." His head dipped. "Even when I'm here, my mind isn't."

"Stand up, Mr. LaPage," said Heather. "Come on this side of the desk."

Brice LaPage looked like a man headed for the gallows. His head hung down and his gaze didn't raise from a spot on the floor. He made it to Heather's side of the desk and asked, "Can I gather a few things before you call security to escort me out?"

Heather gripped his upper arms. "I want you home with your wife. You're on paid leave until you can resume your duties."

His mind seemed to have a hard time catching up to her words. "But... the hotel. The conventions. There's so much to do."

"And I will see that it's taken care of," said Heather. "You have much more important things to take care of."

Heather stepped back. "Would you have Mr. Cruz join us?"

In mere seconds, the assistant manager knocked on the door. He entered and looked at Heather with raised eyebrows.

"Mr. Cruz," said Heather. "You're being assigned as temporary manager. Mr. LaPage will be out for an unknown length of time." She softened her voice. "If you don't feel up to the task, let me know now and I'll get a more senior assistant manager from one of our other hotels."

"No!" He stood even straighter. "What I meant to say is that I'm here to serve however I can. I'll do everything in my power to live up to your expectations."

Heather nodded. "Excellent. Your duties start immediately."

Heather turned to Mr. LaPage. "I'll leave you two alone. If you have any last-minute instructions for Mr. Cruz, make them brief. You're needed elsewhere."

Heather shut the door on her way out. She smiled a mischievous smile as her thoughts turned to security manager Malone. She went upstairs to check on Steve and fill him in on the latest developments.

"You're back too soon," said Steve as Heather walked into the living room. "There's not much to give you yet."

She kicked off her shoes, settled on the couch and sat with legs folded under her, yoga style. Steve's blindness exponentially increased the number of positions she could sit in when she wore a skirt.

"What do you have so far?" she asked.

"Malone's legal name is Rocky Sylvester Malone."

Heather let out a cackle. "You're kidding."

"I'm not creative enough to make up a name like that. His mother must have had a thing for action movies. He's thirty-five, married a half-dozen times and is looking for wife number seven."

"What about credit score?" asked Heather.

"Lousy. In the five-hundreds. He went bankrupt last year."

"Work history?"

"I'm waiting on a call."

"He wasn't ever a cop, was he?"

Steve held up a hand. "Patience. I should get a call any minute."

Heather uncrossed her legs and lay flat on the couch as Steve asked for a report of what she'd learned. She gave details of her talk with Latrice Ohasi. "I also have a thumb drive containing the evidence of girls going to various rooms last night."

"It sounds like she gets paid for looking at screens and not reporting anything," said Steve.

"I think it's more a case of selective reporting," said Heather. "The hotel is well run most of the time. It's clean and occupancy is high. The food can be excellent, but we both know there's something going on in the kitchen. Security seems to handle most things a little more hands-off than I'd prefer, but not all that bad." An empty three seconds passed before Heather added, "That doesn't mean Malone isn't running girls, stealing, or had something to do with Robby's murder."

"When are you going over the books?" asked Steve. "I'll bet there's a lot the hotel writes off as loss."

Steve's phone rang. He spoke for a few minutes, issued a sincere thank you and signed off.

"It seems your hotel security supervisor is under qualified. He's never been a cop, let alone a captain. The closest he ever came to law enforcement was working as an unarmed security guard. That lasted two months before they canned him."

A groan rose out of Heather. "That jerk has his staff call him Captain Malone."

Steve scratched his chin. "His mother's penchant for fiction must be hereditary."

"What about criminal history?" asked Heather.

"That's where things get interesting. He's avoided prison, but should get reward points for frequent stays in the Dade County Jail."

"How wonderful," said Heather. "What's his favorite pastime?"

"Assault. He's a fighter, as long as he knows he can win."

Heather rose from the couch. "This makes no sense. How did Malone get a job as the head of security?"

Steve shrugged. "If I was you, I'd ask the person who hired him."

Heather slumped on the couch. "Speaking of, I sent Mr. LaPage home to take care of his dying wife."

Steve sat motionless and didn't speak. The very mention of a spouse facing death could bring back a flood of memories of Steve's Maggie. She wished she hadn't mentioned it.

"Sorry. That came out flippant."

He waved off her apology, but she knew he'd be thinking about Maggie if she didn't get his mind off her. Steve beat her to it when he asked, "Where's Detective Warner?"

"Taking another lap around the various conventions to check on the food and then to try his luck with interviewing kitchen staff again."

She wanted to make sure Steve's thoughts didn't go back to his deceased wife, so she asked, "Did you hear from Kate's private investigator?"

Steve shook his head. "Nothing but, 'Leave your message after the beep.' I think I'll lay down and listen to Bella's recording of the reports again. There's something about them that isn't right, but I can't put my finger on it."

She slid her feet off the couch on her way to vertical. Steve's voice stopped her in her tracks as she headed for her room. "After lunch we need to find a camera shop."

She looked down at her knees and bare feet. "Do I need to change?"

"Do you want to climb a ladder in that skirt?"

23

———

Scrolling down the images on her phone, Heather announced, "Larry's Camera Emporium is four miles from here. It says he carries cameras to fit your every need."

"Lipstick cameras?" asked Steve.

"Miniature cameras and recording devices. Motion sensitive and continuous play."

Steve nodded his approval.

The cab looked clean enough, and the driver knew where to go. Heather instructed him to wait and promised him cash enough to make it worth his while. He put the car in park, leaned back and pulled the bill of his baseball cap over his eyes. Getting paid to sleep seemed to appeal to him.

Thirty minutes later, the private detectives climbed back into the cab with multiple bags. "Back to the hotel," said Heather to the driver as he yawned and put the car in gear. On the way, Heather pulled four lipstick cameras from a sack and took them out of their boxes. "I'm putting several cameras in your jacket pockets."

"All of them?" asked Steve.

"We'll save a couple for the security office."

"What if Malone's there?"

"Then I'll go back when he isn't." Heather watched as pedestrians hurried to get out of the afternoon sun and into their air-conditioned destinations. Miami stayed warm and sticky, even during the Christmas season.

LATRICE OHASI DREW HER GAZE AWAY FROM HER COMPUTER monitors when Steve and Heather came through the door. Heather made introductions and directed Steve to a chair. He parked himself and threw a leg casually over a knee. His demeanor came across as that of a man without a care in the world. Before long he had Latrice telling an abbreviated version of her life story. Her smile broadened with each mention of her family.

With the ice broken, Steve changed the subject. "I worked as a cop for twenty years. I've never been in a police station or known a security office that didn't have a coffee pot on at all times. Is there any chance you could get me a cup?"

The laugh came from her belly; a hearty laugh, one she'd brought from Africa. "No coffee for me at work. Captain Malone drinks it, but I can't."

Steve's head recoiled. "Why can't you have a cup of coffee?"

"It makes me pee. I can only leave my seat for ten minutes during my shift."

"How long is your shift?" asked Heather.

"From six in the morning until six at night."

Heather hoped her next question didn't sound too sharp. "What about the night shift? Do they work twelve hours also?"

Latrice nodded. "That's my sister."

Heather squatted down to look eye to eye with the ebony-skinned security officer. "Do you need to use the restroom now?"

Latrice looked around with eyes that registered fear. "I can't. I'll lose my job."

Steve answered before Heather had a chance to. "This will be our little secret. Ms. McBlythe and I will stay here. If Captain Malone comes back before you do, we'll tell him Heather gave you permission."

"Are you sure?"

Heather pulled Latrice to her feet. "I'm positive. Don't worry. I'll take care of Malone."

As soon as the door shut Steve said, "You'll have fun taking care of Malone."

"It will be a short, enjoyable conversation." Heather moved to complete the task at hand. "I'll get the cameras set up."

"And I'll watch the monitors."

Steve's self-deprecating sense of humor was a good sign his mind now focused on the job at hand. Memories of Maggie at Christmastime might reappear, but for the time being, he pushed them back into a pretend closet in his mind.

Heather hid the tiny cameras in discrete locations, one in Malone's office and one in the monitoring room. By the time Latrice limped back in, Heather sat gazing at the bank of monitors.

The trip through the maze of hallways that passed by the kitchens and led to the loading docks went without incident. Men with sweat-stained shirts unloaded a lone bobtail truck at the loading dock. They looked as though they could have cared less if a blind man and a woman came on their turf, as long as they didn't impede or interfere with unloading a truck of fresh produce.

Heather found a ladder leaning against the basement's wall and wrestled it to where a distant security camera looked down from a support pillar. Instead of trying to find a discrete place to hide the lipstick camera, she bit off a piece of clear tape from a roll and affixed it to the side of the non-working security camera. She climbed down and repeated the process on a second camera.

With the ladder returned, Heather approached Steve. "All done on this side. Let's go to the other side of the fence where the big shots park their limos."

"Where did you put the cameras?" asked Steve.

"I taped them to the existing cameras. Whoever cut the wires won't think to look there. Everyone else is so used to the camera looking at them, they won't pay it any attention."

"Hidden in plain sight," said Steve.

Before they climbed into a freight elevator, Heather examined the oversized space. "Don't step back once you're in, Steve. There's a puddle of blood behind you."

"There must have been a large meat delivery today. I can smell it."

"Can you imagine how much food it takes to keep this place going?" asked Heather.

Steve shifted his weight as the elevator shuddered to a stop. "They would never miss several hundred pounds on any given day. Over time, someone could live comfortably on what they sold."

Heather led Steve to the right as soon as the elevator door opened.

"Where are you taking me?"

"To the other side of the basement. We have to walk down a flight of stairs."

They arrived in time to hear the metal garage door rattle its way closed at the far end of the parking garage. A loud metallic clang put an exclamation point on whoever left. Otherwise, nothing moved on this side of the fence. Heather looked at the pillar with the security camera mounted on it. She wasn't keen on repeating her tree-climbing routine with Steve playing the role of a squatty oak. She wanted to kick herself for not bringing the ladder.

She cast her gaze around the garage, looking for places that might work. There had to be another place she could mount the cameras where she'd have a view of people coming and going out the door and another to monitor the elevator. A wall-mounted fire extinguisher, several feet from the stairway door would have to do. She brought Steve with her.

"No more tree climbing?" he asked.

"I'm taping the camera to the top of a fire extinguisher. I'll get the profile of whoever comes through the door."

"What about the elevator?"

"That's tricky, but we may be in luck. There's a pole with a no parking sign about twenty feet away. One side is in the shadows but has an unrestricted view of the elevator."

"Put it as high as you can and let's get back to the room." He felt around him with his cane. "What time did you say Detective Warner is coming up to see us?"

"We have twenty minutes to finish. Let's hope he had better luck with his interviews today."

24

─────────

A glass of lemonade awaited Detective Warner when he entered the penthouse. He thanked Heather, and they moved to a bank of floor-to-ceiling windows overlooking the beach. Waves curled and foamed as surfers did their best to get in brief rides. Wind and tide weren't cooperating to make anything but uninspired attempts to push water to shore.

The afternoon crept toward five o'clock so Heather got down to business. "We're scheduled to be downstairs in a few minutes. We promised to make ourselves available to the writers. I'm afraid we'll be busy for most of the evening. If something important comes up, come find us."

"Give him a run-down on what we found out about Captain Malone," said Steve.

Heather scoffed. "Captain. He's never been captain of anything but maybe a rowboat, and it probably sank."

For the next few minutes, she explained Malone's background and the disabled cameras in the basement. She also mentioned the abuse of Latrice and her sister by making them work twelve hours with only one break. Questions and answers played back and forth like a game of tennis. Once again, his pen raced across pages to capture notes.

Steve remained silent during Heather's report. When the conversation petered out, he shifted to the next item. "Heather and I went to a camera store today and purchased enough cameras to cover the loading dock and the VIP entrances into the hotel."

"Are they operational?" asked Detective Warner.

Instead of answering, Heather spun her laptop around for him to see. The screen divided into six smaller screens giving separate views of the basement, including the loading dock, the freight elevator and two points of entrance and egress in the VIP section. "You can see we also placed a couple in the security office."

"Does Malone know about these?" asked Detective Warner.

"Heavens no," said Heather. "The one thing we don't want is him knowing we can see these areas."

"Are you sure he's involved in the thefts?"

"Not yet," said Steve. "We suspect he's being paid to look the other way and keep his mouth shut."

Heather added, "We haven't ruled out his involvement in the murder."

Steve's phone chimed. "Heather and I need to get downstairs. Before we go, I have an idea how we need to proceed. This is only a suggestion, and I'm not telling you how to move forward with the investigation."

"I need a fresh idea. Detective Vance is riding me to get more information from the kitchen staff and they're not talking."

Steve leaned forward. "Heather will focus on the thefts. She needs to get into the personnel files and discover who hired Malone to be the head of security. She also needs to check on the executive chef who goes by Chef Miguel."

"Don't forget Evie Brooks," said Heather. "She purchases for the kitchens."

She added, "I'm ordering a forensic audit of the hotel. That will give us a picture of what's stolen and in what quantities."

With his face turning to Detective Warner, Steve said, "You have the job of getting statements from people who saw Robby the last couple of hours he was alive."

"I'm already on it. I have two other officers interviewing the night kitchen staff as we speak."

"You may need more."

"No dice," said Warner. "The department cracked down on overtime. I was lucky to get the two and only for four hours."

Steve shook his head. "I miss being a cop, but I don't miss the bureaucracy." He drummed his fingers. "We'll make it work. Heather will be busy most of tomorrow and I need someone to be my eyes. But I know who can help me."

Heather tilted her head. "Could this helper be an attractive mystery writer who wears alluring perfume?"

She chuckled when Steve didn't answer. "What about Lara and Kira? Have you made any progress in finding them?"

"That's pretty well wrapped up," said Steve.

"It is?" asked Heather with more inflection in her voice than usual. "When were you going to tell me?"

Steve flicked his hand to dismiss the question. "Such an easy problem. I'm surprised you haven't figured it out yet."

Heather shook her head. Detective Warner placed his hand over his mouth to hide a smile. Heather's incredulity lasted only a few seconds. Seeing Steve hitting on all cylinders did her good. He'd used his time in silence to work out two of the mysteries facing them. His jibe told Heather she wouldn't find out the answer until later, or until she figured it out herself. Fine by her, she had plenty to do.

Steve rose. "Questions?"

"What time do I need to be here tomorrow morning?" asked Detective Warner.

"Eight thirty and come hungry," said Steve.

25

———————

Occasional squawks and guffaws punctuated the drone of hundreds of voices. Heather led Steve into the ballroom and scanned the scene. They arrived late, and it looked like the group had started thirty minutes early on the free open bar.

Heather leaned into Steve when he spoke. "A lively group," he said.

"Nothing like free booze to get a group of introverts loosened up. There's three bars with lines ten-deep."

"Take me to a place where I can hear you better and tell me what you're seeing."

Steve's hand stayed on her shoulder as Heather navigated a channel through the women. They had to stop three times and answer questions on the way. With Steve settled in a chair, she sat next to him.

"Put some chairs facing us," said Steve. "If I'm answering questions for two hours, I want to be comfortable."

Heather did so and said, "I feel like we're bait on hooks, waiting for hungry fish to swim by."

"Don't remind me of fish. It makes me think of Bella. I hope she's all right. I feel bad I haven't had more time to spend with her."

Heather spoke in a loud whisper. "Something's different. Many more writers are congregating in the center of the room. There's still two distinct groups on the edges, but nothing like the first evening."

"Ah," said Steve.

Elissa strolled up and parked herself in one of the two chairs facing them. Heather noted that Elissa looked stunning, even after a full day of seminars and campaigning. What is it about some women? They look like they stepped off the cover of a fashion magazine even after an interminable day.

While Heather played mental gymnastics, Steve said, "Elissa. Glad you could join us."

"How did you know it was me?"

"Your walk and your perfume. Both are distinct and the fragrance smells expensive."

Heather joined in. "I see a lot of women wearing their scarves. How's the campaign going?"

"It's hard to tell. Hazel's storm troopers are passing out buttons meant for their team to wear."

"I saw those," said Heather.

"What do they say?" asked Steve.

Elissa draped a long leg over the other. Her manicured toes sparkled. "Hazel had better luck with the spelling. I have to hand it to her; the buttons are large, bright, and the slogan is simple but effective. They read, *PROFESSIONAL WRITER*. The implication is clear. If you're not on her team, you're not a true professional."

Heather said, "Many of the women are wearing Hazel's button AND the scarf you gave them."

Elissa sighed. "It shows how many are undecided."

The room buzzed with laughter punctuating conversations as lines at the bars slowly diminished. Heather refocused on Elissa. "We were busy all afternoon. Did Lara show up?"

"Not yet," said Elissa with a shake of her head. "She and Kira are still missing."

Steve leaned forward. "It sounds like you need to shake things up if your team is to win."

Elissa crossed her arms. "What do you mean?"

"Come closer. I don't want any of Hazel's people to hear."

With legs and arms uncrossed, Elissa scooted her chair toward Steve. He whispered, "I have news you'll be glad to hear, but I don't want you to tell anyone that I told you about it."

"What is it?"

The crispness in Elissa's voice told Heather the woman across from Steve preferred to live life on her own terms.

"If you don't promise," said Steve, "I won't tell you and you'll lose the election."

Heather bit the inside of her mouth. Steve held all the cards and they must be a royal flush.

"All right," said Elissa. "I won't reveal you as being the source."

Steve gave his head a firm nod and leaned even closer to her. "On Saturday you need to nominate Kira as the next president."

Elissa gasped and her eyes widened. "You found her!"

"Shh," said Steve. "Not so loud." He paused and acted as if he was looking around for spies. "She'll be here in time for the nominations."

Elissa rocked forward and planted a kiss on Steve's cheek. "That changes everything. There's not a woman here that doesn't love and respect Kira. The reign of Queen Hazel will finally end."

"Remember," said Steve. "You didn't hear it from me."

Elissa sprang to her feet after she promised again. She made for her supporters' corner and spoke with a group of women. Hands raised in victory. Women dispersed across the room. The news spread with the speed of a prairie fire pushed by high winds.

Taking a tissue from her purse, Heather set to work at removing lip prints from Steve's cheek. Looking up, she said, "Hold on to your hat, here comes Hazel. I hope you know what you're doing. You won't like it if she puts an enormous lump on your head with that cane."

Steve brushed off the warning with a wave of his hand. "Don't worry. I have this under control."

Hazel made her presence abundantly clear by stabbing the tip of her cane three times into the carpet. The muffled sound contrasted with her sharp tone. "Mr. Smiley. I demand an explanation."

Heather wondered why Hazel hadn't included her in the command for answers. She dismissed the thought and scooted to the edge of her chair with her legs coiled. If she saw the cane raise to strike Steve, she'd be in position to block it.

Steve motioned for Hazel to take the seat Elissa had vacated. "Thank you for coming to see us, Hazel. You saved me a trip and I have wonderful news for you."

Confusion crossed Hazel's wrinkled face. She wobbled and nearly fell forward. Heather sprung from her chair at the same time one of Hazel's lieutenants grabbed the octogenarian's arm. Between the two, they lowered Hazel onto the chair.

"I'm all right," complained Hazel, even though the color had drained from her face. Despite sweat popping up on her top lip, she fought through whatever afflicted her and spoke in a scratchy voice. "Is the rumor true? You found Kira and Elissa will nominate her for president?"

Steve sat back and nodded.

Hazel's petite frame expanded and then contracted as she took in a large breath and released it. "With Lara gone, I don't stand a chance against Kira. It's over for me. A lifetime of work will come to rack and ruin."

"I thought you said Kira is a fine writer and has a level disposition. Don't you think she'll make a superb leader?"

Hazel sighed. "She is the lesser of the evils. Kira isn't a shrew like Elissa, but still, I'd like to leave knowing traditional writers will not be relegated to second-class citizenship."

"I'd like to speak to you privately," said Steve. "Would you grant Heather and me a few minutes alone with you?" He paused. "You'll be interested in what I have to say."

Hazel flicked a hand and her guardian moved away.

The corner of Steve's mouth gave the slightest of quivers. "What would happen if Lara showed up Saturday?"

"Don't tease me, Mr. Smiley. You refused my offer to employ you to look for her."

"No, we didn't. We refused to take your case to find Kira. We told you we'd look for Lara on our own."

A spark entered Hazel's eyes. "Are you saying you found her? Is she all right?"

Steve didn't answer her questions. Like an angler hooking a large trout on a fly rod, he took his time playing out line and reeled her in one turn at a time. After several open seconds he asked, "How would you like to see Elissa sweat?"

By this time Hazel had inched forward to the edge of her chair, balancing herself with the aid of her cane. Heather feared she'd spill onto the carpet.

"You know my opinion of Ms. Lutz," said Hazel. "Propriety is the only thing that's kept me from scratching her eyes out."

"Heather," said Steve. "Can anyone hear us?"

"No one is within fifteen feet."

Steve's crooked finger bid Hazel to come even closer. Once again, he spoke in a whisper that didn't travel far. "Follow Elissa's nomination of Kira with your nomination of Lara."

Hazel stammered, words refusing to form.

Steve continued before she could put a coherent sentence together. "If you tell anyone before the nominations begin, you risk not seeing the look on Elissa's face when you nominate Lara."

Hazel's hand rubbed the handle of her cane as if she were polishing the silver. Her hand stopped. "Where is Lara? I want to see her."

"She's in the hotel," said Steve. "She wanted to make Saturday special for you by making a last-minute appearance. She believes the relief of you knowing she's not harmed will be enough to satisfy you and to sway the election. In the meantime, she wants you to rest and not worry."

Hazel leaned back. A load of immense size seemed to lift from her crooked body. "Lara is such a clever girl. This will end the same way as in her book, *The Missing Duchess*. Only after The Duchess of Southbridge knew the true killer did she reveal her identity and have her day of revenge."

"Remember," said Steve. "Don't tell anyone. You wouldn't want Elissa finding out."

Hazel tried to raise herself from the seat. Heather came to her rescue. The old woman's arm was skin and bone covered by a gauzy blouse. She nodded a thank you. Her aide sped to her side before Heather could beckon for help, and the two shuffled back to Hazel's corner.

Steve put into motion a plan that reminded Heather of a snowball that would turn into an avalanche. News of Lara's discovery met with gasps and cheers. Alcohol fueled speculation of the outcome of the election caused the already boisterous room to erupt into hundreds of noisy conversations. The thrum of the room lowered as the buffet lines opened and plates filled.

Heather brought Steve a plate of thin slices of rare roast beef nestled between yeast rolls with horseradish sauce. She added a few token fresh vegetables for good measure. After he'd finished one of his miniature sandwiches she asked, "Why were you so nice to Hazel? You didn't have to allow her the pleasure of seeing Elissa's chin drop when she heard Lara would be at Saturday's meeting."

"Elissa wasn't nice to an old lady. We elderly need to stick together."

Heather wagged her head. "If you don't produce Kira and Lara, you won't need to worry about growing old. Remember, the people in this room think up ways to kill people."

Heather took a bite of calamari. "Speaking of killing people, I need to do some snooping in the Human Resources office. It doesn't look like we're going to have any more takers on our question-and-answer session. Are you ready to leave after you eat?"

"I've done all the damage I can do here," said Steve.

"I'll drop you off at the elevator."

"Do you see Kate?"

"You two must have telepathy. She's walking toward us."

A slender woman with unkempt hair and wearing two of Hazel's buttons intercepted the hybrid author before she could get to where they stood. "It may take a minute. One of Hazel's supporters is bending her ear." He didn't respond, which wasn't unusual. When Steve drifted to a place of deep thought, he reminded her of a submarine... run silent, run deep.

As they waited, Steve found his voice. "You have things to do. Why don't you run along and solve Robby's murder? I have some things to discuss with Kate."

26

———

Excitement waned as the crowd digested both the meal and the news of the two lost authors. Lowered voices meant Christmas music became audible. Steve's mind went back in time to winter treks to Galveston with Maggie. She loved digging her toes in the sand, setting up her easel and sketching whatever caught her eye. She came alive walking barefoot in the cold briny water. The breezes, along with the sights and sound of crashing surf, became an elixir to her soul.

He complained that the salt-infused air wasn't good for their car. How shallow could a man be? How many moments of fun did he forfeit? What would he give to see her squint in winter's sunshine? If he could see her turn and run into the surf just one more time. If he could... He examined his mental state and blamed it on the music that seemed to grow in volume the longer he stood here.

Melancholy settled in like a thick mist as he stood alone in the company of hundreds. He couldn't shake the memories. Cold winter days. That's when Maggie did her best works as an artist. How did she give a seagull such a lonely, abandoned expression?

Steve ran a hand down his face. He wanted to rid himself of

his self-loathing for not protecting her, but how? His sightless world gave him plenty of time to play *could-have, should-have.*

A woman's voice pushed the spell of Maggie's memory away, if only temporarily. "Steve? Steve? Mr. Smiley?"

"Sorry, Kate," he said, hoping he didn't appear to be a complete dolt. "You caught me lost in thought. Do you mind if we sit down?"

"You look like you could use a stiff drink. Here, I brought you something."

Steve reached out with his left hand and felt a cold, sweaty bottle. "I hope it's something stronger than what I've been drinking."

"Root beer. Heather said you have a taste for it."

Steve thanked her and tapped his way back to his chair while Kate settled next to him. The fragrance settling over him suited her voice: soft, subtle and gentle.

After taking a swig, he lowered the bottle. "The room's getting noisy again."

"Full campaign mode. Two rumors have everyone talking. Have you heard them?"

"Only two? I'm surprised there aren't three." Steve raised his bottle and took another drink.

The seconds of silence told him he'd caught Kate off guard.

"What do you mean three?" she asked. "The ones I've heard say Lara and Kira will go head to head at Saturday's election."

"Did you forget about the murder of Robby Calano?"

"How stupid of me to forget the most important thing you and Heather are dealing with. I've written so many mysteries, I forget I'm living in the real world where horrible crimes aren't something solved between the covers of a book. I must have been channeling my protagonist, Detective Blane Derringer, and how he'd react to the two missing authors."

Steve chuckled. "Do you often get so caught up in your characters that fiction blends with reality?"

"It's a common malady among authors."

Steve rose to his feet. "If you wouldn't mind guiding me through the maze to the elevator, I'm ready to head up to our suite."

"I'd be delighted, sir."

"Lead on, Detective Derringer, or Kate Bridges, or whoever you are."

She laughed. Once again, he noted the timber of her laugh. A merry laugh that seemed to float.

"Left hand on my right shoulder?" asked Kate.

"That works best for me." Steve noted that she stood a little taller than Heather, but not much. They wove their way through the crowd and made it into the hallway. They hadn't gone far when his guide came to a stop.

"Mr. Smiley." The voice belonged to Detective Warner.

"Steve. Call me Steve." He tilted his head toward his guide. "This is Kate Bridges. She's one of the premier authors at the convention. She consented to guide a broken-down former cop to the elevator."

"Hardly old or broken down," said Kate. "It's a pleasure to meet you, Detective Warner."

"I'm a big fan of yours, Ms. Bridges, especially the Blane Derringer series."

Before they could continue, another voice broke into their threesome.

"Mr. Smiley. I hate to disturb you, but I was told Ms. McBlythe is looking for me. I thought she was with you in the ballroom."

"Ah, Mr. Cruz," said Steve. "Have you met the famous author Kate Bridges, and Detective Warner?"

"I met Detective Warner this afternoon. As for Ms. Bridges, it's a pleasure to meet you. I trust your stay is satis-factory?"

"More than satisfactory."

Steve addressed Mr. Cruz. "You must have just missed Heather. She's on her way to the personnel office. Although she's perfectly capable of picking the locks, she'd prefer it if you unlocked file cabinets for her."

Mr. Cruz excused himself. Soft footsteps faded down the hallway. Steve waited until the assistant manager drifted out of earshot. Steve raised a hand to place on Kate's shoulder, then lowered it. "No, I couldn't ask you two to do that."

In unison, both Kate and Detective Warner spoke. "Ask us to do what?"

"It's just a passing thought. Never mind, you both have something more important to do."

"Tell us," said Kate.

"It's just an experiment I've always wanted to conduct. It's nothing."

"No," said Detective Warner. "Tell us and let us decide."

"All right. If you insist." He shifted his cane to his left hand. "It's not every day that I get a police detective and a gifted author together at the same time. In fact, it's never happened. I always wondered who would have the best powers of observation. Heather gave me a sketchy description of the man who just left, Mr. Cruz. I know this is silly, but I can't picture him."

Kate broke in. "Writing unique physical descriptions is something I've worked at for years."

Detective Warner added, "You know I'm trained to document details."

"This might be fun." A grin parted his lips. "Would you two be willing to give me a full, accurate description of Ricardo Cruz? Everything from hair to the soles of his shoes."

"Sure," said Detective Warner.

"I'm up to the challenge," said Kate. "Why don't we put a wager on it? What do you say, Detective?"

He hesitated. "Cops aren't rolling in money. What did you have in mind?"

"I'll mail you an autographed and inscribed copy of the next Blane Derringer book if you win."

"And if I lose?"

She thought for a few seconds. "I'll name my next villain after you. What's your first name?"

"Clay."

Steve laughed out loud. "I can hear the other detectives razzing you now. You'd better write an excellent description."

"I'm going now to write mine," said Kate.

"Before you go," said Steve. "I was wondering if you might have time tomorrow afternoon to take me to interview a few of the kitchen staff."

Kate's voice brightened. "I wouldn't miss it for the world. Call or text me with the time and place to meet."

Steve ended the hallway conference by saying, "Clay, take me upstairs. I have something else you can help me with."

27

The penthouse had a hollow feel as Steve walked in. The enticing smells of Robby's cooking were but a memory, covered now with a sweet, floral scent. No doubt the maid had been there.

Warner's footsteps fell behind him. Steve made for the chair he now claimed as his own and folded his cane. His shoes came off and he reached for the wooden handle protruding from the chair's right side.

Once settled, Steve said, "I have a confession to make."

"Oh?"

"I already have a good mental picture of the assistant manager, but I don't have one of Kate. Would you mind typing something out?"

"Would you rather I type it out or tell you?"

"My laptop will convert the text to speech and I can listen to it several times if I need to." Steve reclined, but not all the way. "Thirty to forty-five minutes of quiet is what I need more than anything. I'll give you the password when you're ready."

"What will you be doing while I'm losing the bet?"

Steve leaned back a little farther. "If you hear me snoring, you'll know I'm not working on the case."

The only sounds were those of the air conditioner blowing chilled air, and the soft, distant thuds of fingers tapping across a keyboard. He needed to think. His mind shifted to Heather. What was she gleaning from the personnel files? Would she have time to discover any irregularities in the books? Her delving into the investigation could put her in danger. After all, Robby's curiosity cost him his life.

He issued a sigh. He couldn't stop Heather, even if he wanted to. The independent Yankee in her would keep her nose on the trail of the killer and the thieves until they saw the inside of a jail cell. He reconsidered his unspoken words. He had used killer and not killers. Was more than one person responsible for Robby's murder? Perhaps. In fact, it seemed likely. Whoever killed him had to move his floppy, bloody body, and that's difficult for one person to do. Stealing large quantities wasn't a one-person job either.

What about Malone? He had the strength and the disposition toward violence.

His thoughts shifted to Bella. His audible groan brought a snicker from the dining room. Clay must have thought he'd nodded off. No matter. How was she coping?

The ding of the elevator brought Steve's thoughts and worries to a temporary end. "You're back early," he said.

Heather greeted Detective Warner and settled near Steve on the leather couch. "I'm back early because there's virtually nothing in Malone's personnel file, including who hired him."

"Interesting, but not unexpected," said Steve. "What about the financials? Did you look at the books?"

"I saw enough to make me suspicious. On Monday, I'll have forensic accountants start a full audit."

Steve moved on. "I'd like to hear from Clay. How did your interviews go today?"

The office chair squeaked, and soft footsteps brought Detective Warner near. "Not great." His voice had a hollow, disappointed sound to it. "I spoke with a dozen kitchen workers.

They're a closed-mouthed group. The dishwashers and prep-cooks kept their heads down and worked while giving me one-word answers. They seemed scared to say anything. The chefs were just as bad. It looked like they got together and decided how they would handle the questioning. They all spoke louder than necessary and said they knew nothing. I gave each of them my card. It surprised me when I received a text from one of them. She'll talk, but not anywhere near the hotel."

"Excellent," said Heather. "All it will take is one that's willing to give up information. The rest should fall like dominoes if she gives us enough."

"We have to be careful with that," said Steve. "It could be someone trying to shift the blame onto someone that isn't involved."

"I thought of that," said Clay. "I'll follow up first thing in the morning."

"You said the chef is a woman?" asked Heather.

"During the initial interview, she said she hasn't worked here long and made a big deal of not knowing much about how the place runs. I'll run background on her before I set up a meeting."

"Do it now on the laptop," said Steve. "If she can meet with you and Heather tonight, you'll have a good jump on the day tomorrow." He paused long enough to get a breath. "What about custodians? Have you spoken to the staff responsible for cleaning the hallways, the freight elevator, or the dock areas? Janitors and housekeepers blend into the background. People forget about them, but they have eyes and ears just like anyone else."

"Not yet," said Clay. "I thought I'd start on that tonight before I go home."

Steve shook his head. "Leave those to me. You and Heather have a hot lead. If the chef can meet you tonight, having Heather along will allow you to play good-cop, bad-cop."

"I'll be the good cop," said Heather. "I can promise her things like rapid advancement or transfer to another hotel if she fully cooperates."

"And I can hint there's no shortage of empty jail cells if she won't cooperate," said Clay.

Steve added, "Word is out one of the board of directors of the hotel is here. Heather's presence should be enough to loosen her tongue."

The leather couch creaked softly as Heather rose to her feet. Steve heard her move to the office, and clicks of the computer keyboard sounded.

"We still have a feed to the garage," said Heather. "We need someone to monitor it tonight."

"Clay, could you call vice and have them send someone?" asked Steve. "Working girls are using the elevator in the VIP parking garage to gain entrance to the hotel."

Heather added, "We're not interested in them, but we need to know who in the hotel is running them."

Clay made the call after saying there'd be a fight to see who won the lottery to come to the penthouse. Spending a shift in a luxury hotel suite watching a computer monitor with your feet up didn't happen every day.

His next call went to the chef who said she wanted to talk. She agreed to meet and gave the name of an all-night diner miles away from the posh hotels of Miami Beach.

The elevator door closed behind Heather and Clay, leaving Steve alone until Bella arrived, most likely in a flurry of teenage energy.

When Bella arrived, she ordered from room service and watched the computer monitor while they waited for vice to show up. All remained peaceful until the house phone rang. It had been so long since he'd heard a landline, Steve wondered for a moment what it was.

"Can you get that, Bella?"

After muffled sounds, she approached with quick footsteps. "It's the assistant manager. He must have thought I was Heather and didn't give me a chance to speak. We're to go to room 407. He said it's urgent."

28

Steve never liked Alvin and the Chipmunks, especially their Christmas album. He rested his hands on his cane, wishing for sound deadening headphones until the elevator doors retracted. Bella tentatively led him down a carpeted hall, stopping after a few steps.

"Where's Ms. McBlythe?" The effeminate lilt to the voice made Mr. Cruz's voice distinct.

"Thanks for calling," said Steve. "I'm afraid you mistook Bella for Heather."

Bella broke in. "You didn't give me a chance to say anything."

"What's the problem?" asked Steve.

Mr. Cruz's voice cracked. "I'm afraid one of our guests has expired."

"Is anyone in the room?" asked Steve.

"Our director of security, Mr. Malone."

Steve directed his words to Bella and Mr. Cruz. "We need to get him out of there."

The door clicked and Steve jerked it open. "Get away from the body. Touch nothing and come out in the hallway."

The smells of beer and sweat followed Malone. Steve spoke before he had a chance to say anything. "I can tell you've been drinking. The police will be here any minute. It would be best for your future employment if you disappeared and drank a pot of coffee. They'll want to talk to you after they secure the room, so don't leave the hotel."

Footsteps headed toward the elevators. Steve hollered. "Take the stairs!"

The assistant manager relayed a second useful piece of information. "The occupant of the room is an attendee of the mystery writers' convention, Hazel Smallgrass. I received multiple calls from concerned friends asking us to check on her well-being."

Implications of Hazel's death raced through Steve's mind. He puffed out his cheeks and released a deep breath of air. How many would blame Elissa? Could she be responsible? Was he dealing with a second homicide or had Hazel succumbed to the inevitable effects of time?

"I heard the door to the room close," said Steve. "I need it opened again."

Mr. Cruz slid around him, and the door lock made a whirling mechanical sound. Once inside, Steve told Bella to make sure the door closed behind them.

Steve took in a shallow breath. "Say the name, Hazel Smallgrass."

"Huh?"

"We don't have time for questions. Trust me and say her name."

"Hazel Smallgrass," said Bella.

Nothing. Steve breathed a sigh of relief. "This is what I hoped for. She died of natural causes."

Bella cleared her throat. "I don't mean to sound rude, but how can you be sure?"

Steve knew the question would come. He contemplated letting her in on his secret, but that would only complicate things. The medical examiner would come to the same conclusion he had, and with cops on their way, he didn't have time to explain. Bella would have to take him at his word.

He launched into questions of his own. "You don't see any signs of violence, do you?"

"No."

"And everything is neat and organized?"

"Well, yes, but—"

"Go to the nightstand. There should be several medicine bottles, or they might be in the bathroom. Without touching them, read the labels."

Bella's soft footsteps stopped after about ten feet. "One is for Metroprolol Tartrate, another is Atorvastatin, and one is for something called Amioderone."

"There should be another small bottle."

"There's one on the floor. I can't read the label, but tiny pills spilled from it. I don't think I've ever seen pills so small."

"Nitroglycerine tablets. All of those pills are to treat a heart condition. She must have been reaching for the nitro when her heart gave out." Steve sighed. "Let's get out of here."

The door clicked shut behind them. Soft footsteps approached. The scent of perfume hit him at the same time Kate's words did. "What's happened to Hazel?" Extreme concern propelled the words as her fingers gripped his forearm.

Steve answered the question with one of his own. "Were you coming to see her?"

"Yes. She had a flare up after you left. I saw her place a tiny pill under her tongue. I tried to talk to her, but her associates said she needed to get to her room and rest. She didn't object."

Steve placed a hand over Kate's. "Hazel's dead."

Her grip intensified. "No. She can't be. Everything was going the way she wanted it to. You convinced her that Lara would show up and clinch the election."

Steve patted her hand. "Then she died happy. What else can we ask for?"

The first officers arrived on the scene and Mr. Cruz met

them halfway down the hallway. Steve leaned into Kate. "Go on to your room. If the police ask, I'll tell them you were curious, and I told you to leave. There's no need for your name to be in a report."

The officers had little to do except secure the area and take preliminary statements. Like so many deaths, the investigation would be short and efficient, especially after Steve told them his background, and he was working with homicide and vice on unrelated cases.

After Steve gave his account to the officers, he turned to Bella. "Let's get back to the penthouse. The guy from vice should be here soon."

The trip upstairs brought new thoughts to Steve. The election of new officers for the mystery writers' conference would take place on Saturday. Wild speculation about Hazel's death would spread like a plague through the mystery writers, and these were people with fertile imaginations for murder.

He pushed the thoughts into a file in his mind and closed it. One thing at a time, and that one thing was the murder of Robby Calano. What would Heather and Detective Warner glean from the chef they traveled to interview?

29

The first challenge Heather and Detective Warner faced was getting from Miami Beach to Miami. Every road funneled onto a causeway. Guarded by the Atlantic Ocean on the east and The Everglades National Forest on the west, Miami traffic has its own unique problems and runs primarily north to south. It doesn't move fast or far if you head west. North-South isn't much of a bargain, either.

After twenty minutes of weaving through traffic on I-95, Heather let out a sigh of exasperation. Until then, conversation had been sparse. Both seemed content to allow the miles and the crazy drivers to pass by without comment.

"Another ten minutes and we'll be there," said Detective Warner.

"You never told me this woman's name. What's she like?"

"O'Quinn. Margaret O'Quinn. You'll like her. She's unique."

"That could mean many things. Do you think she'll be truthful?"

A boyish smile crossed Warner's face. "I'm glad you're with me. She'll be honest with you, but I don't think I'd be able to get much out of her." He shot her a quick glance. "She's short, stout, and sassy, if that helps."

After acknowledging the answer, Heather withdrew into herself. Detective Warner wanted Margaret O'Quinn to be a surprise. Perhaps he didn't want to influence her questions. She'd soon find out.

Her thoughts shifted to Steve and the surprising relationship percolating between him and Kate. Was he growing fond of her and her for him? Had she done the right thing in leaving him alone at the party and again by coming with Detective Warner? She could justify it because she had a responsibility to the hotel. It might be a legitimate reason, but she didn't like leaving Steve alone while working on a murder case.

They took an exit off the interstate and passed under it, heading west. Heather didn't catch the name of the street, but it must have been a significant artery because it stretched four-lanes wide with a median. Three blocks down, they pulled into the parking lot of a diner that looked like it had been around since Eisenhower sat in the White House.

The racially diverse clientele included a group of blue-jean-clad workers, hip-hoppers with baggy shorts and scrubs-wearing nurse's aides. Detective Warner wore the only necktie in the room.

"There she is," said Detective Warner. "The last booth on the right."

Heather scanned down the row of booths covered with something made to look like leather, but the plastic sheen told the truth. Her eyes locked on a head that appeared to be covered with French-cut carrots, spiky, orange, and shining with gel. The woman definitely stood out.

Leading the way, Detective Warner nodded a greeting and introduced Heather. She scooted in the booth while extending her hand and shaking one that reminded her of a lobster's tail with fingers tinted red and scarred from burns, the telltale sign of a practicing chef. The woman had small, sharp, green eyes set in a round face that looked like it could laugh with abandon or cuss like a dock-worker, as the occasion demanded.

The chef took in Heather with an appraising eye and ignored Detective Warner. "They told me you were hot." The words came straight from a part of Boston not known for residents afflicted with an Ivy League education.

Heather took on the persona she'd used when she worked as a detective with Boston P.D. She leaned forward and spoke in a brogue almost as thick as Margaret O'Quinn's. "And I hear you're a talented chef that wouldn't mind a promotion." Heather leaned back. "I'm rich and I'm pretty. So what? You're Irish as a leprechaun and you can cook. Now that we've got that out of the way, I understand you're willing to talk to us about what's going on at the hotel."

"I might," said Margaret. "First, I want to know what you think the Red Sox chances are against the punks in pinstripe this year."

The question was part of a social game played by Bostonians, a way of feeling out people to see if you could trust them. The amount of information conveyed by Margaret would depend on how Heather responded. She shook her head and gave an expression intended to project hopelessness. "It'll take help from every saint in the book. We had two good left-handed relievers. One had Tommy John's surgery, and the other got traded last week. For what? A utility infielder and a draft choice. If they don't get someone with a catapult for a left arm, things will be ugly."

A firm nod of Margaret's head didn't budge the five-inch spikes of hair. For the first time, she looked at Detective Warner. "Ask your questions. I'll tell you what I know."

Further discussion halted when the waitress brought coffee and glasses of water.

"I hope you wanted coffee," said Margaret. "It's the only thing I'd recommend in this place."

The waitress responded by sticking out her tongue, a sure sign Chef O'Quinn and the server were on a first name basis.

After opening a black notebook and pulling out his pen,

Detective Warner turned to Heather. "You take the lead. I'll follow up if I need to."

Heather looked at Margaret. "I'll start with a couple of questions, but they're only designed to get you started. You've got a brain and a tongue." She paused. "I haven't looked at your personnel file yet. How long have you worked at the hotel?"

"Almost three months."

"Who hired you?"

"The manager, Mr. LaPage, and Chef Miguel."

"That's not his real name, is it?"

Margaret smiled. "It's Miguel Moreno. He's from the south side of Chicago. White Sox territory."

"Is he involved in the stealing that's going on?"

The ping pong of questions and answers slowed as Margaret hesitated. "I don't think so." Her red eyebrows folded in toward each other. "He's too focused on his cooking to be much of a thief. He insists on preparing the meals for the VIP guests in the most exclusive restaurant."

"Does he oversee the ordering of supplies?"

She shook her head. "Each chef submits a requisition. It goes to Miguel's administrative assistant. She's responsible for making sure we're well stocked."

"Are you?"

She shrugged. "It depends. The hotel's restaurants are exceptional. The food varies for the conventions. Sometimes they serve pre-packaged muffins taken out of plastic and placed on a fancy platter. Other times, it's decent."

"What's the administrative assistant's name?" asked Detective Warner.

With only a glance his way, Margaret said, "I think her name was Eve or Evie or something like that. Everyone calls her Miss Sunshine."

"Why's that?" asked Heather.

"It's a joke. She looks like a professional lemon-sucker.

Everyone avoids her. I drop off my requisitions in a box by her door. All the other chefs do too, including Chef Miguel."

Heather would look into Miss Sunshine when she returned to the hotel. She could be the brains behind the thefts, but what about the brawn?

"Does Miss Sunshine ever have company in her office? Does she pal around with anyone?"

"Like I said, she ain't social."

O'Quinn anticipated Heather's next question and continued, "I'm told the stealing takes place on the loading dock in the basement. That's where supply trucks make deliveries. They load the food on the freight elevator and cart it to the kitchens one floor up. I hear some gets left in a walk-in cooler in the basement."

"Why the cooler in the basement?" asked Heather.

Margaret stirred her coffee, but didn't drink. "It makes sense if trucks run late."

Heather looked out the window. "All it would take is a padded requisition. Someone working the dock could check off everything as delivered. But not all the supplies ever make it to the kitchens. Free merchandise sold at wholesale or retail. That's a high-profit business plan."

"You catch on fast."

Heather shifted her gaze back to O'Quinn. "Any idea about who's carting off our supplies?"

Margaret shook her head. "Sorry. I've never been to the dock. One chef did, and they fired him. The only reason I know so much is he told me what was going on before they sacked him."

"I'll need his name," said Detective Warner.

Margaret balked. "Wait a minute, cowboy. I don't want to lose my job or end up as fish bait. That nosy New York kid found out the hard way. Whoever's ripping off the hotel plays for keeps."

Heather took over. "It's time for you to decide. You can give us the name of the other chef or find a new job. I'm not partial to people who don't have a backbone."

"That's the thanks I get for talking to you?"

Heather leaned forward and stared. "I can be very generous when I'm properly motivated. Give us the name and call in sick tomorrow. Expect a pay raise on your next check. If you're still not comfortable working there, I'll get you transferred to one of our other hotels."

Margaret leaned back. "Must be nice to be rich."

"You'll be a little closer to knowing what it's like if you give us the chef's name."

She did, along with a phone number.

Heather had another thought. "What kind of guy is this chef that lost his job?"

"He's an awesome chef, even if he is a Yankee die-hard."

Heather couldn't help but smile. Who'd have thought her love of the Red Sox would be her ticket to cracking the case. "I'll be staying in Miami longer than I expected. I'd like to meet your chef friend. Do you think he can come to the penthouse tomorrow morning and cook breakfast for us?"

O'Quinn had a shocked look on her face. "I can call him."

"Do it," said Heather as she looked at the oily shine on her coffee and decided the water looked to be the lesser of two evils.

It took several minutes of convincing, but after some salty cajoling, O'Quinn convinced him.

Heather had one more thing to tell the woman. "Wash that goo out of your hair and fix it like you're going to a convention at the hotel. Call your chef buddy back and tell him you'll pick him up bright and early. He needs to wear business casual and so do you. I want both of you in the penthouse by seven. You'll prepare breakfast for six. Nothing fancy."

"You're a woman I wouldn't mind cooking for full time."

Heather nudged Detective Warner and scooted across the seat. "I take that as a high complement."

They made for the exit and into the thick night air. Once

back on the interstate, Detective Warner asked, "Do you know who killed Robby Calano?"

"Not yet. I need to run everything by Steve. It will surprise me if he doesn't have everything figured out."

"Care to tell me?"

Heather smiled and looked away. "A famous detective once told me I needed to be patient. He'll be waiting on us to give him a report."

30

A bleary-eyed Detective Warner dropped Heather at the hotel's front door at 10:30 p.m. She scurried past the front desk, anxious to inform Steve of the interview.

A woman's laugh floated from the living room when Heather entered the penthouse. Of all things, she didn't expect there to be laughter. A disheveled man sat at the dining room table with the remnants of a sandwich and a steaming mug in front of him. He nodded a greeting and gave his name, something long and bloated with consonants. He wore the look of a vice officer: clothes from a dumpster, the baseball cap of a team that habitually lost, and a beard in need of a trim.

Heather strode into the living room, eyeing Steve in his chair, still grinning from whatever he told Kate that caused her to laugh.

"You're back from your scavenger hunt," said Steve. "I was telling Kate about how you showed up at my door after your father had you kicked out of Houston's police academy. There you were, worth hundreds of millions, but you couldn't get your mitts on any of it until you turned thirty. We were a twenty-first century remake of the odd couple."

Kate couldn't contain a giggle. "Months away from a king's

fortune, but you didn't have money enough to make rent. Such a hilarious irony."

"It was hilarious alright." said Heather.

"And you told Steve you couldn't move in with him unless Max came with you. He thought you meant some guy you hooked up with, not your cat." Kate looked up with a smile that caused the corners of her eyes to crinkle. "I can spend ten minutes with Steve and get enough fodder for a full chapter in a book."

Kate composed herself. "Please forgive me. I didn't mean to make fun of your situation, but I needed a laugh after what we've been through tonight."

Heather grimaced. "Glad my life story gave you a reprieve, but a reprieve from what? What happened?"

Steve explained. "You and Detective Warner had already left when I got the call from Mr. Cruz. Hazel died in her room this evening."

"What!" Heather's mind raced. She'd been so busy with the affairs of the hotel and Robby's murder, she'd all but forgotten about the feud dividing the mystery writers. "Was there any sign of violence or foul play?"

"Natural causes," replied Steve.

Steve's answer had a ring of certainty to it, but she couldn't help but ask, "Are you sure?"

"He's sure," said Kate. "He won't tell me how he knows, but he lost all interest in her death after he and Bella went into Hazel's room. I've never known a detective or a policeman that didn't want to wait for an official ruling."

It struck Heather like a freight train. Steve went in the room and heard Hazel's name. He used his gift of associative chromesthesia to rule out homicide.

Did he tell Bella? Heather considered the question and concluded he hadn't. She and his former partner, Leo, were the only ones who knew about his gift. Steve wanted to keep it a secret because it would have been too much of a hassle to explain.

Heather leaned back. Hazel died of natural causes, but would her supporters believe Elissa didn't have a hand in her demise?

A voice erupted from the dining room. "Ms. McBlythe, you'll want to see this."

Heather bolted out of her chair and circled behind the vice officer. A covey of underage teens exited the elevator in the VIP section of the underground garage.

The officer keyed his radio and informed his cohorts. His eyes closed as he concentrated on the reply coming through his earpiece.

"Where will you take them down?" asked Heather.

"A few blocks away. We couldn't tie up all our resources by having people wait around all night." He stood. "We owe you for giving us the tip and having the camera setup. Do you want to come along for the show?"

"Go with him," said Steve. "Kate and I will stay here. She can monitor the loading dock until Bella gets back from dancing. She went out with her sponsors." He paused. "How did your meeting go? Have you solved the murder?"

Heather shouted from the elevator. "We'll talk when I get back."

THE ABSENCE OF HEATHER AND THE VICE OFFICER LEFT THE penthouse eerily quiet, the way a theater feels when you're the last one to leave. Steve focused his attention again on Kate. "Are you ready to experience the glamorous side of being a detective?"

"You want me to stare at a computer screen?"

"I'd forever be in your debt." He knew his response to be hyperbole, but it did the trick. The hybrid mystery author rose from the couch and padded her shoeless way to the dining room. Steve rose and followed.

The dining room chair made virtually no noise when Kate settled on it. Steve sat next to her, close enough to enjoy the subtle wafts of fragrance drifting his way.

"Not much of a plot," said Kate. "I'm staring at multiple views of a loading dock with not a soul or truck in sight. If this gets any more exciting, I may need a seatbelt."

"You don't find it scintillating with nail-biting suspense and intrigue?" asked Steve with all the seriousness he could muster.

Kate chuckled in a high, simple note that reminded him of one of the middle bells in a bell choir. "This is where I'd condense time in my story. Something like, 'The image on the screen never changed. Hours passed without so much as a wayward gray mouse with a white belly, making his late-night rounds to forage.'"

"That's good. I can see him scurrying and stopping to look around. He's sniffing and then his head jerks up. His ears twitch. He bolts for cover."

"You should write. I bet you have a unique authorial voice."

"Speaking of writers," said Steve as a way of changing the subject. "Who will be the new president, now that Hazel's gone? Do you think it will be Lara or Kira?"

A huge sigh came from Kate. "Poor Hazel. She gave so much of herself. She..."

A triplet of sharp inhales found his ears, the telltale sounds of sniffling. His question must have opened the gates holding back tears. He sat without talking, waiting for another wave of grief to pass. He still experienced those waves from time to time. They had a nasty habit of showing up with alarming frequency during the Christmas season. As if on cue, his wife Maggie appeared in his thoughts. One of the many disadvantages of being blind was he couldn't open his eyes and allow another image to take her place. So, there they sat, a private detective and a mystery writer, both being washed over by waves of grief.

Steve came out of his trance when Kate blew her nose then asked him how he would spend Christmas. It took him aback and forced him to concentrate. "I'm not sure. I thought of finding somewhere to go, but Heather sprang this conference on me at the last minute. Last year was great. Bella's parents invited us to stay at their resort in the U.S. Virgin Islands. I buried myself in audio books and escaped almost all the hubbub of the season."

He hoped his next words didn't sound like self-pity. "Heather promised her parents she'd visit them in Boston. I told her I didn't want to go. I guess I'll stay home with Max." He tried to sound cheery. "What about you? Holidays with the family?"

"No family. I'm starting a new series. It's a police procedural mystery which will be out of my comfort zone. I'll probably hole up in my office doing research and banging away on my laptop."

"Ahh."

"What does that mean?"

"It's a sound I make when I want to acknowledge I heard and understand, but I don't want to say what's on my mind. It comes in handy when questioning suspects."

Kate responded with her own, "Ahh."

The elevator dinged, and the doors whooshed open.

The hotel manager on duty said, "Mr. Smiley I brought Detective Warner. He said he needs to see you."

"Yes, thank you for escorting him up." The elevator doors whispered shut.

"Come in, Detective," said Steve. "You've met Kate. Heather and the vice officer are interviewing ladies of the evening, and Bella's somewhere in the bright lights of Miami." Steve paused. "I thought you were going home."

"I thought I was, too. Detective Vance wants me to monitor the video screens and make an arrest if I can."

"That's my cue to leave," said Kate. "It's been a long day and tomorrow promises to be eventful. I'll be playing peacemaker between the trads and the indies. There's no telling what rumors will fly around the conference concerning Hazel's death."

"Another death?" asked Detective Warner. "Here at the hotel?"

"Natural causes." said Steve.

As Kate retrieved her shoes, Steve asked, "With Hazel gone, who will win the election?"

Her footsteps stopped. "Good question. If Lara shows up, she'll take it."

"What if both Lara and Kira come on Saturday morning? It sounds like they need a talented hybrid author to be a neutral third party to run the election."

"Ahh," said Kate. "Good night, Detective Warner. Good night, Steve."

"That's a classy lady," said Detective Warner once the elevator door closed.

"That's not all she is," said Steve in a voice that didn't rise to the level of conversational speech. He changed the subject and the tone of his voice. "Keep an eye on Heather's computer screen. You're looking at the loading dock. I'm not expecting anything tonight, but who knows. You may get lucky."

As the detective settled in, Steve gave details of the evening's activities, starting with Hazel's death.

"Is it just me or does there seem to be a lot going on in this hotel?" asked Detective Warner.

Steve wondered again if everything was connected. The murder of Robby, the thefts, the call girls. Too much to be a coincidence. Like a jigsaw puzzle, he could see a pattern in the colors, but the pieces didn't fit. At least not yet.

"Tell me about the interview you and Heather had with the chef," said Steve.

"Margaret O'Quinn," said Detective Logan. "You'll meet her in the morning. She and a chef they fired for being nosy will be here to cook us breakfast."

"Thank goodness," said Steve. "I was afraid Heather would try to cook. At this stage of the investigation, I don't trust room service."

"Do you think we're close to knowing who killed Robby Calano?"

Steve considered the question, but not for long. "Ask me again tomorrow morning, about eight-thirty. In the meantime, keep watching the loading dock. If you nod off, don't worry about it. Heather set it up to record. Bella should be back soon and you two can work out a schedule. She's a night owl, so she'll probably want the first shift. That might be an opportunity for you to go home and get ready for tomorrow."

Steve stood and issued a boy scout salute. "I'll be in my chair if you need me. I need to think."

"Or sleep?"

31

T he annoying sound of the alarm on her cell phone jolted Heather from what amounted to a nap instead of a night's sleep. She'd tried a dozen different ring tones, including a buzzer, instrumentals, Broadway show tunes, and one that shrieked, "This is your mother. Get up!" Her latest, the opening guitar riff of *Sweet Home Alabama,* sounded better than most, but not this morning. Waking up fully clothed on top of her bedcovers and desperate for a toothbrush didn't help matters.

Twenty minutes later, she followed the smell of freshly brewed coffee into the living room. A fluffy hotel bathrobe covered her freshly scrubbed body while a terrycloth bath towel, wrapped around her head like an Arabian turban, corralled her hair. The world would have to take her as-is until she could repair the damage done by so little sleep. She plopped, more than sat, on the couch near Steve. He chuckled softly.

"Glad I could bring a little humor into your morning," said Heather.

A mug of black stimulant appeared directly in front of Heather, as if by magic. She looked at the stubby fingers offering it and then to the round face framed by a startlingly attractive head of soft, short red hair. "Is that you, Margaret? I didn't recognize you without the rabid porcupine look."

Margaret clucked her tongue and quipped, "Speaking of wildlife, you have the look of a raccoon about you this morning. Do you want this coffee, or would you like a little hair of the dog?"

Heather took the mug. "I wish I could blame my looks on having an enjoyable time. I worked until my body rebelled and this is my less-than-three-hours-of-sleep look."

Heather stared at Margaret's well-coiffed hair and worked her way down. Makeup had taken the splotchy redness out of her face. She wore a green blouse accented with a Christmas themed scarf and straight-leg gray slacks that had a slimming effect. The chef cleaned up well.

The sound of banging and clanging pans cut through the morning stillness until the door closed again behind the chef.

Steve sat in silence until Heather downed her coffee, one of the many informal agreements between them. Coffee before conversation. He honored the pact until the sound of the mug settling on the end table reached his ears. "Short night?"

"Short and restless. My mind whirled like a Ferris wheel."

"We must be near the end. Your mind goes into high gear when you've been productive. Start with the shady ladies and go from there."

Heather fortified herself with a yawn and a stretch before she launched into her night's activities with vice officers. "The women left in a rented limo. The driver didn't know or care who he transported. He's at the bottom of the food chain and gets paid by the hour. The officer that was here last night will call me later this morning and let me know who owns the company."

"Don't expect much," said Steve. "The person paying the bill is most likely using an alias and a pre-paid debit card." He took a sip of coffee. "What about the girls? Did you get anything useful from the interviews?"

"That proved productive," said Heather. "I singled out the

one that looked the most frightened. The cops agreed to make a deal with her because this was her first arrest. They released her after she gave us the description of their boss."

"Malone?"

"She picked him out of a pile of mug shots."

"I knew he had to have a side hustle of some sort going on."

Heather spoke through a yawn. "Vice will pay Mr. Malone a visit this morning... right before I fire him."

Steve lowered his feet. "Ask them to hold off. Have them come to the mystery writers' meeting tomorrow morning at ten-thirty. Your job is to get Malone there."

Heather stared at Steve. The corner of his mouth nudged up ever-so-slightly. That minute gesture gave her all she needed to know. "Partner, you have a wicked look about you."

Taste buds came alive when the smell of fresh-baked biscuits reached Heather. Her stomach made a growl of anticipation. Again, Steve chuckled. He derived untold pleasure from her gastronomical eruptions. She responded with a terse, "Hush. I can't help it."

With a murder investigation still to settle, Steve changed the subject. "You didn't get home until after four. Surely you didn't take that long with vice."

"I went back to the personnel office. Malone's missing paperwork got me to thinking there might be others. I pulled the files on everyone we and the police have interviewed. I got carried away and looked at most all the files of current employees."

The sound of the elevator door opening interrupted the conversation, which suited Heather. She needed a second cup of coffee.

"Pardon my appearance," said Heather as she greeted Detective Warner. "I've not had my sixth cup of coffee yet."

Detective Warner responded with a yawn.

Chef O'Quinn exited the kitchen with a carafe and sat it on the bar along with cream, sugar and extra mugs.

"Thanks, Margaret," said Detective Warner. "You look different today."

Once again, she clucked her tongue. "You'd better hope this coffee puts some starch in your shorts. You look done in."

With mugs full, Heather and Detective Warner took a seat in the living room. The sound of Steve's voice jerked Heather back from her thoughts. "Detective Warner, I thought I heard you leave in the wee hours. Did you see something or give up and go home? If you did, Heather can fast-forward and see if anything happened around the loading dock."

"You..." He stopped and cleared his throat. "Sorry I'm not good and awake yet. You and Bella missed the show, and I almost did. I lifted my head off the table in time to see someone wearing a hoody carry a box from the walk-in cooler on the back dock and put it in the back of a panel van. I got the license number and name of the company. It's B & E Restaurant Supply. I'm having trouble tracking the owner. It looks like a dummy company with an answering service. The physical address is a post office box in a UPS store. That's as far as I got before I went home for a shower and a change of clothes."

"You didn't call it in?"

"I've been up forty of the last forty-eight hours and my brain feels like overcooked Ramen. I could tell from the radio traffic that it would be impossible to get patrol units to respond, and I didn't feel like getting chewed out by Detective Vance for missing the collar."

Bella chose that moment to saunter in from her room, digging sleep from the corner of her eye. She plopped down beside Heather, hugging an oversized pillow which gave a greater measure of modesty to her sleep shorts and t-shirt.

Heather squinted one eye. "Did you paint the town red again?"

"We went to two clubs, but I wasn't in the mood for men hitting on me. Me and one of the few women executives took a walk on the beach and talked; mostly about how sorry men can be." She looked at Steve and the man next to her. "Present company excluded."

The kitchen door flew open. Chef O'Quinn moved with the determined motion of a robot on a fast-moving assembly line. She scattered plates, silverware, napkins and glasses on the dining room table, then spoke as she scurried back to the kitchen. "Breakfast is coming out and chefs don't like it when people disrespect them by allowing food to get cold."

The group didn't need to be told twice. Despite her frenetic movements, Margaret had set the table to perfection. Green aprons covered the fronts of the two chefs who appeared with serving dishes of breakfast meats, crepes, six choices of sweet breads, cottage fried potatoes, a mountain of biscuits and sausage gravy. Sliced mangos, sectioned grapefruit halves and fresh-squeezed orange juice rounded out the meal.

Chef O'Quinn made an abbreviated introduction. "I'm bad with names, so you can introduce yourselves to Chef Stephan while we eat."

Stephan, a bear of a man with a thick reddish-brown beard and a stomach that competed with his chest for circumference, nodded a greeting. "I apologize for the meager fare. If I'd had more time and a few more ingredients, we could have made something more eclectic."

"You've done very well, Chef Stephan," said Heather. "And you, too, Chef O'Quinn."

Bella slid into a chair beside Heather and fell upon the feast like a ravenous jackal. Her white-blond hair hung equally divided over each shoulder and spilled onto her lap. She ignored Chef Stephan's stare, reached for a cinnamon roll, and shoved a good portion of it in her mouth. Despite fame, fortune, poise and polish, she was still a seventeen-year-old girl.

Conversation ceased, at least until Steve put down his fork. "Bella, what does your morning look like?"

She pushed a bite into the corner of her mouth, making her look like she had an abscessed tooth. "Not much. They set up a gigantic fish tank in the exhibit hall and we're taking turns doing casting exhibitions. Also, they're having a drawing for prizes, including an eighteen-foot boat that comes with a Mercury two-hundred motor and trailer."

"Good," said Steve. "How would you like to say hello to a thousand mystery writers?"

She shrugged as if it were no big deal. "Sure. That would please the publicity people from the movie studio. Can I pitch the film?"

"The film and the book," said Steve.

Heather wasn't sure Steve had clout enough to set the agenda for the writers but held her tongue.

"What about you, Detective Warner?" asked Steve.

"I need to interview the janitors and maintenance workers."

"If you can, leave your afternoon open. If all works out the way I think it will, you'll need to get at least one search warrant."

The breakfast continued until, one by one, forks, knives and spoons lay across empty plates. Bella excused herself and slipped away to her room. Steve nodded in Heather's direction, his sign that she needed to glean information from Chef Stephan.

"Thank you both for such a wonderful meal," said Heather. "I'm sure Margaret told you why we wanted to talk to you."

Chef Stephan gave a nod to Heather and made eye contact with Detective Warner. "It's about me getting fired because I was too inquisitive."

Heather pushed her plate forward. "Before we get too deep into this, why don't you tell us about yourself and how you came to work at this hotel."

For the next several minutes Chef Stephan summarized his upbringing, education and culinary experiences. The breakfast proved Stephan to be a talented chef. Also, he had a degree in accounting and years of experience managing the kitchen at a major hotel in the area. He'd been let go when new management took over the hotel and didn't agree to keep his salary at the same level.

Detective Warner made notes as Heather continued. "It's our understanding they fired you because you went to the loading dock. Is that true?"

"Partially true. I was used to overseeing all aspects of the kitchen. That included ordering supplies, overseeing preparation, and making sure the servers kept on their toes. The double accounting system I use tracks profits and losses. I keep my books and a bookkeeper double-checks everything and pays the bills. I'm also a big believer in annual audits by a CPA. I found things were different here. They compartmentalize the bookkeeping. Chefs cook, servers serve, dishwashers wash dishes and all ordering and receiving is one person's responsibility. Questions aren't welcome, and there's no one with an overall view of the operation."

Heather tilted her head. "What about the executive chef?"

Chef Stephan looked away, as if he wanted to take time and choose his words carefully. "You'll not find a finer chef in the world to prepare signature dishes. He's amazing, and I learned so much from him in the brief time I was here."

Heather lifted her eyebrows, "I sense your opinion of Chef Miguel comes with reservations."

He squirmed in his chair. "He's a superb chef, but that's the extent of his skill set."

Heather meant to follow-up, but Chef Stephan went down another path. "Like I said, I came from a more holistic background. I wanted to know how the customers reacted to the food we served. Not just my food but the food from other cooks, sous chefs and specialty chefs. So, I'd slip out of the kitchen from time to time."

"What did you discover?"

"I talked to the other chefs individually. I got a sense of what they were ordering. Then I looked at what was being served, especially to the conventions. Things didn't add up."

"Did you tell Chef Miguel about your concerns?" asked Steve.

"Yeah, I told him. He said he'd send a memo to management. I guess he did because I got chewed out."

"By whom?" asked Heather.

"Which time? First by the Assistant Manager, Mr. Cruz. Then by Miss Sunshine, whatever her name is. She's the woman who's supposed to do the ordering. Finally, that excuse for a hotel detective lit into me."

"Malone chewed you out?" asked Heather.

He gave a firm nod. "He tried to give me the gangster treatment, but I told him to back off."

Steve cleared his throat. "You didn't stop complaining, did you?"

"I've been around kitchens a long time. I don't mind employees filling up a plate and going on break, but I draw the line at stealing unprepared food."

He shifted his gaze back to Heather. "I knew what was being ordered and what made its way to the conventions. I went to the loading dock in the basement to find out if all the orders made their way to the kitchens. The next thing I know, I'm escorted out of the hotel by that jerk Malone."

Steve pushed back from the table and stood. "Thanks for answering our questions and cooking such a wonderful meal. If you're free this morning, I'd like you to be our guest at the mystery writers' convention. That includes you, Chef O'Quinn."

Margaret rose and began gathering dirty dishes. "We didn't get dressed up for nothing." Her eyelids narrowed, like she didn't trust Steve. "Tell me you don't want us to stand up and talk in front of everyone."

"Stand up? Yes. Talk? No."

For the first time, fear shone in her green eyes. She and Stephan gathered dishes and ferried them to the kitchen.

Detective Warner left without fanfare as he had interviews to conduct. Music played from behind Bella's closed door. That left Heather and Steve alone at the dining room table.

"You have everything figured out." Heather intentionally

phrased it as a statement and not a question. It didn't surprise her, even though it left her flummoxed that he was a step ahead of her.

"Not quite everything," said Steve.

"When were you going to tell me?"

"I need you to open up your computer. We need more background on people to have enough for Detective Warner to get search warrants. Then, I'll tell you who killed Robby and who's behind the thefts."

"Aren't you forgetting something? What about the missing mystery writers, Lara and Kira?"

He met her question with a sly smile. "I'll save that one for later. The answer has been right in front of you all along." Steve took a sip of coffee to hide his grin.

Heather retrieved her laptop and fired it up. For the next hour, she and Steve investigated hotel employees. Phone calls to well-placed individuals in Florida and Texas filled in any gaps. By the time Heather closed her lap top she and Steve knew the people they were investigating better than their mothers.

"There's one more thing I need you to do tonight," said Steve. "Rig up a video camera with sound in one of the unused breakout rooms and have it ready to feed into the room where the mystery writers meet for their general session. Hazel sabotaged the schedule, and we weren't able to give our seminar on interrogations. Tomorrow we'll give them something to remember."

"What will we do the rest of today?" asked Heather.

"Wait and lie low," said Steve. "We also need to double and triple check everything to make sure I'm right."

Steve had the situation under control, but something sprang up in her mind that caused pain deep in her soul. His keen mind had unwound another tangled mess of clues and people would go to jail. But what about afterward? With the dreaded Christmas season upon him, being left alone at home for weeks might cause Steve to unravel. She'd learned from his former partner that he'd begged for the pistol he carried as a detective. She also knew he'd come within a trigger pull from using it the Christmas after Maggie died.

Heather stared at the man she admired. She needed a plan. What could she do with Steve to take him away from haunting memories? She needed to think of something fast.

Another thought crossed her mind. The participants of the writers' convention would learn today their leader had died. How would they react?

32

Steve's cane swept left and right as Heather led him over carpeted hallways with Christmas music playing through hidden speakers. He didn't flinch or groan, a sign that his mind had locked on the tasks at hand. The distant roar of voices, some sounding like faulty brakes, sharp and grating, increased the closer they drew to the mystery writers' conference.

"Take us to Kate," said Steve.

The meeting, six minutes shy of being gaveled into session, crackled with the static electricity of suspicion. They approached the front of the stage where Kate and the woman Heather recognized as the secretary of the writer's group stood. Kate wore muted dreary colors, low heels, and stood with shoulders straight, bearing the appearance of grief with a veneer of resolve.

As Heather and Steve approached, she heard the organization's secretary, the next in line to oversee the meeting, exclaim, "I can't... I can't do it!" Sobs followed. "Even if I knew how, I just can't."

Kate rested a hand on the woman's shoulder when gasps of grief escaped. The woman shredded remnants of tissues, their pieces falling like soggy snowflakes.

Steve said, "Kate, you need to take over."

The WMWA secretary's countenance assumed the look of a condemned prisoner who'd received a last-minute pardon. Her eyebrows pinched together in a question. "Can she? Is it legal?"

"Perfectly legal," said Heather with unbound confidence. "According to parliamentary procedure, the chair can surrender the gavel whenever they cannot conduct business or when they deem it necessary or appropriate."

Heather wasn't sure if that was accurate, but she learned in law school that you can get by with most things if you sound like you know what you're talking about. "All you do is strike the gavel three times and tell the group you've chosen Kate to chair the meeting."

Steve added, "By the sound of things you'll need someone who's respected by both sides."

A boxcar of worry seemed to lift from the woman's shoulders. "Please, Kate. Please take over. Do it for Hazel."

Kate sighed. "If that's what you want."

The woman turned. "I need to sit down and collect my thoughts. What if I say something wrong?"

Kate walked the woman to a nearby table and deposited her in a chair. She returned and stood looking at Steve. Heather hadn't noticed it before, but Kate had an expression of fondness on her face. It wasn't on her countenance, but in her eyes when she looked at Steve.

Steve had both hands on the top of his cane. "I have a suggestion," he said.

"Will it bring a semblance of order to this mob?" asked Kate.

"I believe it will. First, I want you to introduce us, Detective Warner and Bella Brumley. We spoke with him a little while ago and he's on his way. The medical examiner has officially ruled Hazel died of natural causes. That information coming from a police official should go a long way to calming this crowd."

Heather took over. "As for Bella, she can't stay long today, but she'll be able to come to tomorrow night's banquet. She'll sign copies of her book for anyone that wants it."

"That sounds good," said Kate. "Please be ready to come to the stage after I make some opening remarks."

Steve set his feet shoulder-width apart. "That's not all. I think I have a way of giving them something else to think about."

"Oh?"

"I know many of your writers incorporate food in their plots. Heather hired two chefs to cook for us this morning, and they have plenty of time on their hands. She'll set them up in the hallway to answer culinary questions your authors might have."

"Perfect. The cozy mystery writers will love it, as will many others."

Heather added, "I'll be in the hall if you need me." She patted Steve on the arm and wished him luck.

Steve listened for Heather's footsteps as she walked away, but between the carpet and the crowd, he had to guess when she traveled far enough so she couldn't hear. He lifted his head in Kate's direction and cleared his throat. "There's one other announcement I need to make today."

"Oh?"

"I'm telling everyone that Kira and Lara will be here tomorrow."

She remained silent for a few seconds. "What else will you tell them?"

"I'll leave that up to you." He let the words hang in the air.

"Heather doesn't know?"

Steve shook his head.

"Mr. Smiley, you're almost enough to change my opinion of men."

Soft lips brushed against his cheek.

HEATHER STOOD BY THE DOOR WITH THE TWO CHEFS. AFTER relinquishing her responsibilities, the secretary turned the meeting over to Kate, who set the tone by calling on Detective Warner to give the official announcement of the cause of Hazel's death. She followed this up with a prayer for unity and peace that lasted a full five minutes and evoked quiet sobs throughout the hall.

Following a reverent "Amen," Kate squared her shoulders. "I know many of you feel the way I do at this moment. I'd prefer to go back to my room, bury my head in a pillow and grieve. But having known Hazel all my adult life, I'm afraid that would be enough for her to come back and give me a sharp rap across the backside with her cane." A murmur of agreement rose and died away. "I can say with absolute certainty that Hazel's greatest desire would be for each of you to get the maximum benefits from this conference and not waste a moment. With that in mind, we have some special announcements this morning."

Heather listened to Steve and Bella as each made their announcements to the crowd. The writers rose after being dismissed and she nodded to the two chefs. "So far, so good. Enjoy your day answering questions."

THE SHUFFLE OF FEET DIMINISHED UNTIL ONLY THE MUTED voices of a few stragglers remained. Steve, now off the stage, smelled Heather's perfume. "Is Kate still here?"

"She's walking toward us now," said Heather.

"Thank you both for salvaging the conference," said Kate. "The writers are frothing to speak with Bella, and the two chefs have a line of ladies waiting to pick their brains."

"Good," said Steve. "Perhaps we can give them a special treat tomorrow morning."

"Oh?"

"Heather and I will spend the day confirming our suspicions and gathering evidence with Detective Warner. Tomorrow we propose to give a demonstration on interview techniques. How would your writers like to see an interview in real time?"

"How would you do that?"

Heather answered. "I'm setting up a camera in one of the unused breakout rooms. We can pipe it in to the meeting."

"Are you kidding? That would be wonderful."

Steve added, "If we hit a brick wall today, we can still grab some hotel employees and conduct fake interviews. It might take most of the morning. Are you sure it won't disrupt the convention?"

He felt two hands grasp his upper arms, placing Kate directly in front of him. "Don't you dare cheat these writers out of such a unique experience. This will be a once-in-a-lifetime opportunity."

Steve swallowed hard as a wave of scent swept over him. She released her grip as Heather said, "I'll get with you later today and go over the logistics. In the meantime, Steve and I have a ton of things to take care of."

33

The next morning, following another belt-straining breakfast, Steve followed Heather's lead through the Christmas trees and entered the noisy ballroom. Kate's voice became clear as they neared the stage.

In a quiet tone, Heather gave her an update. "I set a camera up in a room down the hall. A hotel employee will be our suspect in the first demonstration. We'll make the interview as realistic as possible."

"That sounds perfect. We'll dim the lights and it'll be like going to a movie. The only thing on the morning agenda was to hold the election, but that won't happen until right before the noon break. I heard Elissa rallying the independent authors. She's planning on pushing several people to the microphone to give campaign speeches for Kira."

Heather interrupted. "Did Kira show up?"

"I don't see her," said Kate. "Lara is still missing, too, but if Steve say's they'll be here, I'm sure they will." She let out a deep sigh and glanced at the steps leading to the stage. A hand reached out and covered Steve's, still perched atop his cane. "Wish me luck."

Steve gripped Kate's hand but spoke to Heather. "Could you excuse us?"

"Sure," said Heather.

He knew this violated an unwritten rule of their partnership, but he had to settle something with Kate before the day progressed any further.

It didn't take long for the ambient noise to swallow Heather's footsteps.

"I don't have much time," said Kate.

"You need to make time."

"I'm not sure I like the tone of that last statement."

In his mind's eye, Steve could see Kate bristle. He hoped he wasn't going too far with what he needed to say.

"Well? Say what you need to say," said Kate.

"You know where Lara and Kira are. This election is a well-orchestrated plan of your making. Who have you chosen to be the next president?"

Confrontations often cause long pauses in conversations. This one lasted much longer than most, but at least Kate didn't lie. With thorns in her voice, she replied, "I don't see how that should concern you."

"No? You hired us to find Kira. I have."

"You're right. I hired you. Now I'm firing you."

Steve took a half-step forward and lowered his voice. "A nice, talented, and, from what I hear, lovely lady once said something I'll never forget. 'Sometimes a little deception keeps small mistakes from becoming big regrets.' That doesn't apply to big deceptions."

Steve turned and walked until Heather's perfume came into his space.

"Let's get out of here," said Steve. "How much time do we have until our first guest arrives?"

"He's in the hallway waiting on us. Bella's keeping him occupied."

"Perfect. I'm counting on you to take care of him if he comes across the table."

———

MALONE STOOD IN THE HALLWAY LOOKING LIKE HE'D CASHED in a winning lottery ticket. In front of him stood Bella, showering him with attention. He slicked back his hair with an open palm and laughed at something she said.

Bella wore a baggy sweatshirt and skinny jeans tucked inside brown boots with two-inch heels. A thick rope of braided hair cascaded over her shoulder, making her look like a modern-day Scandinavian goddess. The pulled-back style showed off baby-smooth skin.

Approaching the duo, Heather said, "Thanks for showing up Captain Malone. We need your help."

He gave her a look that communicated he didn't care for the interruption. "What do you want?"

The pained look on his face told her Malone belatedly realized who addressed him. Heather acted like she hadn't noticed the crisp tone. "Mr. Smiley and I are making a video for the mystery writers. It has to do with police interviews." She paused. "Did you know we both used to be police detectives?"

"Uh—"

Heather careened on before he could answer. "We need you to be a criminal suspect and we'll pretend to interview you. You know, just like we've already taken you downtown."

"Why me?" A bead of sweat appeared on his upper lip, which didn't necessarily mean guilt. Some men sweat a lot and Malone was one of them. Heather still noted it.

Steve answered, "You're the head of security, aren't you?"

"Yeah."

"We want this to sound authentic. You're a professional and you know how crooks think and talk. I bet you've heard every lie there is."

"I don't get it. What do you want me to do?"

"It's simple," said Heather. "We'll try to get information from you and you pretend to be someone with something to hide." She flashed a smile. "With your experience in law enforcement and private security, it will come naturally."

Bella chimed in, "How cool. Will you interview me?"

Steve and Heather looked at each other but said nothing. Malone gave a husky laugh. "Honey, with your looks, nobody would believe you could do anything wrong."

Bella stuck out her bottom lip. Heather said, "It might be best if you sat this one out."

"Don't worry," said Steve. "You'll get your time in the spotlight tonight."

"Cool," said Bella. She turned and left without another word. Malone's unblinking eyes followed her retreating form until she melded into the forest of Christmas trees.

Sounding like the director of a play, Heather said, "Let's get started." On the way to the conference room, she spoke to Malone in a volume loud enough for Steve to hear. "Once we enter the room, the camera will be running. Remember, this is to look authentic."

A room, slightly bigger than a middle-school classroom, opened before them. Three padded chairs sat on the far side of a utilitarian table with a single metal folding chair nearest the door. Behind the table stood a camera on a tripod. A bearded man wearing a ragged baseball cap swung the camera to capture images of the group as they entered. A microphone sat in the middle of the table.

Heather guided Steve to the far side of the table and settled him with the camera looking over their shoulders. The man behind the camera came forward and pointed to the lone chair facing Steve and Heather.

"Sit," he commanded.

Malone complied.

The man said, "I'm Detective Chevaskowsi with the Miami Police Department." He gave the rest of a standard preamble that identified the date, time and names of persons present. Then he returned to the camera and said nothing else.

Heather and Steve fixed their expressions to appear as solid as the presidents on Mt. Rushmore.

"Captain Malone," began Heather. "You've been advised that you are not under arrest but you are being detained in connection with your involvement in human trafficking. Do you understand the rights?"

He nodded, adding a swarthy grin.

"Please state that you understand."

Slumping in the chair, he tilted his head and said, "Sure, babe. I understand."

Heather continued after she knew he'd taken on the character he thought they wanted. "Mr. Malone, I have your personnel file. I want you to verify that the information in this file is correct." She launched into a series of benign questions, all designed to elicit a simple affirmative response.

Steve took over. "It's our understanding you're responsible for the security cameras in the hotel. Is that correct?"

"Yeah, what of it?"

"And this includes those in the basement?"

"Well..."

"Why aren't any of them working?"

"That's something maintenance will have to answer."

"Are you saying you contacted maintenance?"

"I told one of the girls to do it."

"Why didn't you do it?"

Heather broke in. "It's not unusual for a supervisor to delegate things. Let's move on."

The good-cop, bad-cop routine progressed with Heather asking another softball question. "Mr. Malone, we received a complaint from a former worker at the hotel." She opened a file and looked down. "Here's a photo of a man I believe you know as Chef Stephan. He's claiming termination without just cause."

"I don't remember anything about that incident."

"He contends you escorted him from the building. Is that correct?"

"Oh, yeah. I remember him now. I showed him to the door. That's my job."

"Who fired him?" asked Steve.

He shrugged. "Beats me. All I know is I got a call to walk him out."

"Who called you?" Steve's question hung in the air.

"I don't remember."

Heather opened another file folder. "I can answer that." She flipped through a few pages with a puzzled look on her face. In reality, the folder contained daily schedules of the mystery writer's meetings. She held it so Malone couldn't see what it contained. "The assistant manager, Mr. Cruz, called you. It says he fired Chef Stephan and he called you to escort him out. Is that accurate?"

"Yeah."

"Where's your report of the incident?" asked Steve.

The perspiration on Malone's top lip became more pronounced. "I don't know. I sent it in."

"Don't worry," said Heather. "All reports of this nature are submitted electronically. We can get it off of Mr. Cruz's computer."

Malone squirmed in his seat.

"Mr. Malone," said Steve. "Talk to us about the stealing from the kitchens."

"What stealing?"

Steve slammed his hand on the table hard enough to bounce the microphone a full inch. "Don't play dumb! The stealing that cost Chef Stephen his job because he complained about it. The stealing that you knew about when you threw him out."

Heather knew Steve had planned the slap of the desk, but it made her jump all the same. She watched for Malone's reaction. His eyes had the look of a caged animal, shifting back and forth, looking for a way out. He offered a weak, "I know nothing about stealing from the kitchens."

Steve leaned over the table. "You're the security chief of a major hotel with hundreds of employees and you know nothing about thefts of food worth hundreds of thousands of dollars? Are you saying you don't know what's going on around here?"

Malone tensed. His response came across as overly self-assured. "I know plenty about what's going on." He eased back in his chair. "In fact, I know more about what's going on than anyone else."

This is what Heather and Steve had hoped for. Malone's bragging painted him in a corner. He didn't realize his words would come back to haunt him.

Heather broke the residual tension when she asked, "Who hired you, Mr. Malone?"

The question caught him off guard, and he responded with a questioning gaze.

Heather spoke with as much of an uncaring voice as she could muster. "The only reason I'm asking is that your hiring documents are missing from your personnel file."

The response came back fast. "Mr. LaPage and Ricardo Cruz hired me."

"That sounds right," said Heather. "I'd expect the hotel manager and assistant manager to fill such an important position." Heather took a three second pause, allowing tension to melt away.

Steve asked, "Is it your job to keep the hotel management informed of any illegal activities going on in the hotel?"

"That's right."

In another sudden change of direction, Steve asked, "What can you tell us about the woman working in food service named Evie Brooks?"

By the pink glow of Malone's face, Heather knew the question hit home. So much so, that he made another critical error. He lied. "I never heard of her."

Steve pounced. "Do you expect us to believe that you don't know the woman who processes the orders for food that amounts to over a million dollars a year?"

He haltingly answered, "Okay, I've heard of her, but her office is down in the kitchen area. I don't go there."

Steve held up his hands. "First you said you didn't know Evie Brooks. Now you know her and you know the location of her office." He lowered his hands and leaned forward. "You've been told to steer clear of her, haven't you?"

He didn't allow Malone time to respond. "What can you tell me about a truck that came to the back dock two nights ago? They took at least fifty thousand dollars' worth of food from the walk-in cooler. We're looking for someone to pin it on."

"I know nothing about it."

"You said you knew everything that goes on around here. Now you tell us you don't know anything. Which is it?"

Malone became indignant. "You can't know what goes on in the basement. The cameras down there don't work. You're trying to set me up."

Heather held out her hand. It contained the lone remaining lipstick camera that she didn't mount in the basement or in the security office. "Ever seen one of these?"

His nostrils flared. "Yeah. So what?"

"You keep digging a deeper hole for yourself," said Steve. "Here, I'll give you a shovel. A man went to the basement Wednesday night. Someone shot and killed him there. Why didn't you come to the scene?"

"I... well... I thought it was something for the police to handle and—"

Steve cut him off. "Video footage shows you walking fast down the hallway that runs past the kitchens shortly after Robby Calano was murdered in the basement. That puts you one to two minutes away from where they found his body. How do you explain that?"

"I went to get a sandwich from the kitchen. Plenty of people saw me. Go ask them."

Heather joined in. "You're not helping yourself, Mr. Malone. Even if you got a sandwich, you could have done that on your way back from killing Mr. Calano. It sounds like you're trying to establish an alibi."

Malone sprung from his seat. His face had gone from pink to crimson. Drops of perspiration dripped from his nose. "I didn't kill that kid. I was nowhere near the garage."

Heather patted the table. "Sit down, Mr. Malone." Her soft voice had its effect. He lowered himself, found a handkerchief in a pocket of his jacket and mopped his face.

Heather folded her hands on the table in front of her. "There's one more thing we need to cover. You're running call girls in the hotel."

Steve took over. "Show him the lipstick camera again, Heather." He waited a few moments to make Malone sweat a little more. "Ms. McBlythe set one of these up in the VIP parking garage. The police have footage of underage girls coming out of the VIP elevator. Several of them picked your photo out of a stack with similar physical descriptions. You arranged for them to be picked up and dropped off by a limousine. The police know how much customers paid them and what you pocketed. As we speak, your home is being searched and your bank records are being examined."

Heather added, "The girls thought you'd put on weight since your last police mug shot. I'm afraid there won't be any more late-night trips to the kitchen for free food."

Malone's shoulders sagged and his head lolled like that of a newborn child.

Steve spoke in a firm voice. "Malone, you're going to jail. The man who read you your rights is a vice officer. If you're telling the truth about not being directly involved in the thefts or the murder, you might get by with lesser charges."

"I'm an attorney," said Heather. "If you were my client, I'd advise you to tell everything before the others hang you out to dry. Don't fool yourself. We know everything about the people you're thinking about lying for. They'll say or do anything to save their skin. Have your lawyer make a deal. There's enough evidence to put you in prison for manslaughter and grand theft if you don't."

Steve threw a thumb over his shoulder. "That officer watched the girls get off the elevator and into the limo. He'll take you into custody now."

Malone sighed heavily, shaking his head back and forth.

After handcuffs ratcheted shut, the room became eerily quiet. Steve and Heather rose from their chairs and made their way down the hallways, through Christmas trees and into the writers' conference. All heads turned their way as the room erupted in applause.

Heather wondered if the writers thought Malone's arrest was play-acting or the genuine thing. Either way, act one came to a close, with act two ready to start after a short intermission.

34

If eyes could speak, Kate's would whisper words of admiration as Heather and Steve approached the podium. Heather looked again at the de facto leader of the mystery writers' conference and realized the woman's wordless praise focused on Steve. After an initial rush of jealousy, Heather grabbed her pride by the scruff of the neck and mentally told it to get lost. After all, Steve had once again put a jumble of clues together. Yes, others had done much of the legwork, but it took him to make sense of it all.

After the crowd gave another round of applause, Kate asked Steve to say a few words. That's exactly what he did... said only a few words of thanks and promised the day had only begun. He turned the microphone over to Heather.

She waited for Steve to take a couple of steps away from the podium. "Before we conduct other interviews, Steve and I would like to introduce a very special young lady. You may know her as a television personality, or perhaps you read her memoir that's being made into a major motion picture. She's graciously worked us into her busy schedule this morning." He paused. "Ladies and gentlemen, please welcome Miss Bella Brumley."

A thousand pairs of eyes shifted and a sense of pride rose in

Heather. Even though Bella lived with her for only a month last Christmas, a bond formed that would last a lifetime. The relationship between Steve and Bella was even closer. He'd given her the best gift ever, reuniting Bella with her parents. Heather would give her family fortune if Steve could see the girl that had so thoroughly captured his heart.

Steve spoke in a loud whisper. "Let's go. Bella knows what to do."

"Wait," whispered Heather. "She's almost here."

Long legs carried Bella up the steps to Steve. She gave him a two-armed hug that lasted long enough for some in the audience to applaud. Pulling Steve along with her to the microphone, she tried to speak, but only squeaked out, "This is the best man I've ever met."

The more tenderhearted in the crowd fumbled in their purses for tissues.

Steve leaned into the microphone. "If you'll excuse us, Ms. McBlythe and I have work to finish." He squeezed Bella's hand and took a step away.

Bella cleared the rattle from her voice, and the seasoned professional articulated her words to perfection. "Unfortunately, I only have a few minutes to share my experiences of being kidnapped as a child and groomed to be a television personality. However..." She held the word for effect. "I'll be here tonight after your last session. My publisher has arranged for a shipment of my memoir to arrive this afternoon. I'll personalize and autograph copies for as long as it takes. Also, Mr. Smiley and Ms. McBlythe will be with me. They've also agreed to sign copies."

Heather and Steve approached the door. Elissa rose from her chair and walked toward them. As usual, she looked like she'd stepped off the glossy page of a fashion magazine. She'd gone all-out for the pending election and struck the perfect balance between ultra-chic and business-professional. The sensuous peek-a-boo hairstyle was abandoned for one that pulled her ebony locks away from her face. She'd also toned down the Lamborghini-red lipstick.

Elissa held the door open and followed them into the hallway. "Might I have a moment of your time?"

"Elissa," said Steve. "I was hoping we'd bump into you this morning. How are you?"

"I'm impressed."

Didn't Elissa know she wasted fluttering eyelashes on Steve? Heather concluded it must be a habit when trying to angle something from a man.

"Thanks," said Steve, "but we don't have much time. You want to know if we've found Lara or Kira." It wasn't a question, but a simple statement of fact.

"Well, yes. We're all curious."

"We know where they are, but I can't say for sure if they'll show up for the election. I hope that answers your questions. Please excuse us."

Steve didn't allow her time to respond. The nudge on Heather's shoulder propelled her forward.

Detective Warner eased beside Steve and waited until they had traveled far enough down the hallway so inquisitive ears couldn't hear. "Everything's set up the way you wanted it."

Steve grunted his approval.

DETECTIVE WARNER UNBUTTONED HIS SPORTS COAT, revealing a badge affixed to his belt. The assistant manager, Mr. Cruz, sat in the same metal chair Malone vacated earlier. Unlike Malone, he wasn't a soggy sponge of sweat.

Steve led out while Heather sat with hands on her lap. "No need to be nervous, Mr. Cruz. We only need you to answer a few questions."

Heather gave the assistant manager a hard look. "What Mr.

Smiley means is, there's no need to be nervous as long as you don't lie to us."

"The camera behind us is on," said Steve. "It will stay on until we're finished with you. If I detect anything that falls short of what they call the truth, the whole truth, and nothing but the truth, our interview will conclude. Understood?"

Detective Warner added, "If that happens, I'll read you your rights and we'll handle this in a more formal and unpleasant way."

Heather asked, "Do you know about Mr. Malone's arrest?"

Cruz placed both hands flat on the table. "The police took him on the longest route possible, through the lobby and out the front door. And, might I add, good riddance."

He looked down. "Please forgive the outburst."

"You're happy he's gone?" asked Heather.

The assistant manager straightened his posture. "He's been an embarrassment to this hotel ever since his first day."

"That's an odd thing for you to say since you were involved in his hiring," said Steve.

With both hands, Cruz pulled the front of his sports coat down to take out any wrinkles. "I was in the room. I signed my name. That doesn't mean I approved."

"Didn't you voice your opinion?" asked Heather.

His gaze pleaded for understanding. "I gave my opinion as vehemently as I dared. It fell on deaf ears."

Steve grunted like he remained unconvinced while Heather moved the interview to the next issue. "I have some questions about the employees' records."

"I knew you would. You want to know why there's a separate file cabinet for the food service workers and certain other employees. Those aren't my responsibility."

"Keep going," said Steve.

Cruz lifted his chin a millimeter or two. "There's a division of labor. I'm responsible for the employees in housekeeping, main-tenance, reservations, transportation and the front desk."

Heather nodded. That explained why critical documents were missing, but not for everyone. She looked up from files on the table. "The security director's file lacked a criminal background check. Was his work history verified?"

"It was not."

"Can you explain?"

"Like I said. Those files and the personnel they represent are not my responsibility."

Steve tapped on the table two times. Heather understood. "That's all the questions we have for you, Mr. Cruz. You can return to your duties."

The assistant manager stood, gave a nod, and turned to leave. Steve stopped him with one more question. "Mr. Cruz, do you ever wear Allbird shoes to work?"

He gave the haughty look of an English lord. "Absolutely not. I like to think of myself as a hospitality professional. I'd be most uncomfortable wearing something so inappropriate."

Detective Warner turned off the camera, went to the door, and looked down the hallway in both directions. Steve spoke as soon as Warner returned. "I need you two to go back to the writer's conference. Bella should finish any minute. Tell Kate we'll start the next interviews in twenty minutes. That'll give them time for a break before our next guests arrive."

35

Now alone, Steve rose from his chair and paced. He used his cane to chart a path from the table to the nearest wall, turned and reversed course until he turned at the wall on the opposite side of the room. He folded his cane and stuck it in the pocket of his jacket for subsequent laps. He needed quiet. Revealing Robby Calano's murderer would be easy, but extracting a confession that would hold up in court was another matter.

In their meeting that morning, he and Heather and Detective Warner discussed several methods of extracting a confession. Since none of the plans seemed foolproof, they couldn't agree.

After completing ten minutes of laps, Steve reached in his pocket, withdrew his cane and flicked his wrist. The cane unfurled and became rigid. He walked with a determined stride back to the table where he seated himself and sent a voice text for Heather and Detective Warner to come back.

"This will be tricky," Steve began. "Heather and I can't play good-cop, bad-cop with these two. They're too smart."

"Are you sure you don't want me to take them into custody and finish compiling the evidence later?" asked Warner.

Steve's head gave only a slight shake, showing he didn't want that. "Sometimes it's best not to be a cop. There are things Heather and I can do that you can't."

"Like what?"

"We can stretch the truth without fear of internal affairs coming after us. We need to walk the fine line between unsavory and illegal. We also don't have the authority, or the obligation, to advise someone of their rights. Finally, private detectives take photos and videos of suspects without their knowledge. It only becomes an issue when used as evidence in court. Some states allow this while others don't. Either way, it's how we get at the truth."

Warner scratched his chin. "You realize that Florida is a two-party consent state, don't you?"

Heather nodded. "I researched the Florida statutes, and this is a room where there's no expectation of privacy. The video camera is in plain sight and I'm one of their supervisors. According to Florida law, employers may record their employees in the workplace for legitimate work-related purposes such as preventing theft or other acts of misconduct."

Steve leaned forward. "What we can't have is you or any other member of law enforcement in the room. It would tip them off that we're on to them and they'd demand an attorney."

"I don't like it, but I see what you mean," said Warner. "What do you want me to do?"

Heather answered. "Go to the mystery writers' meeting and watch. Be ready to come to our rescue when we get a confession out of them. We'll be on the big screen, so use your best judgement when to come arrest them."

Warner took in a deep breath and let it out. "There's been one more development. My senior partner sent me a text. Vance completed his three-day forced vacation. He told me not to do anything until he arrives and takes over. He thinks you're conducting the interviews on the stage at the conference."

"Who gave him that idea?" asked Heather.

Detective Warner tried not to smile, but it only resulted in a cheesy grin. "Let's just call it my work-around."

"How much time do we have?" asked Steve.

"Depends on traffic. Somewhere between thirty minutes and an hour."

"That might be long enough."

"Be careful," said the detective. "I'll post an officer at the end of the hall."

"Not until after they're in the room with us," said Steve. "They're coming voluntarily. We don't want them spooked."

THE DOOR SWUNG OPEN, BRINGING STEVE TO ATTENTION. "It's not time yet," he whispered. "Did they arrive early?"

Bella's voice rang out. "There you are. I looked in every room on the hall."

Steve issued an audible sigh of relief as Bella prattled on. "I wanted to let you know I got a text. A guy scheduled to show techniques for saltwater casting had to cancel. They need me at the bait-casting demonstration pool this morning. I'm on in twenty-five minutes."

"Don't leave yet," said Steve. "Heather, go to the camera and make sure it's working. Use Bella sitting on the other side of the table to make sure you have the frame set properly."

"I need to scoot," complained Bella.

"This will only take a few seconds," said Steve.

He turned to Detective Warner. "Tell Kate to give the group a fifteen-minute break."

The two departed at the same time.

"Any last-minute instructions?" asked Heather.

When Steve didn't answer she knew he'd once again retreated to that private place within himself.

Heather used the time to rearrange chairs, with two on each side of the table. She made sure the video and audio functioned properly. After completing those housekeeping chores, she settled beside her sphinx-like partner.

Time passed as if someone had drugged it. Heather lived in a world of frenzied deadlines and down time affected her more than Steve. He had a hard time remembering the day, let alone the time, unless they were on a case. The transformation to partial omniscience fascinated her.

Heather checked her watch as the sound of muffled voices in the hall brought Steve's head up. Seventeen minutes had elapsed since Detective Warner left. She rose in a rush and met the man and woman halfway across the room.

"Thank you for coming," said Heather. She made sure her voice conveyed friendly hospitality. "I know you're busy, but there's something important we need to discuss. It's about Mr. Malone, the head of security."

Brice LaPage, the hotel manager, gave a nod of acknowledgement. Evie Brooks stood rigid as a flagpole.

"Please," said Heather. "Let's not be so formal. Why don't we all sit down and have a chat?"

Evie settled on the edge of the seat. Brice LaPage also sat rigid, but at least he sat with his back against the chair.

"Why is there a camera?" asked Evie.

Steve flicked his wrist like he was shooing away a fly. "Do you know Bella Brumley?" He didn't wait for them to answer. "Bella's a television personality and she was being filmed in here earlier this morning. Something to do with the fishing exhibition that's going on."

Heather added, "I believe the camera has a flashing red light that shows when it's on. Do you see a red light?" She knew they didn't because none existed on that camera. She moved on as they both stared over her shoulder. "Let me get right to the point," said Heather. "The police arrested Mr. Malone this morning. We want to talk to you because they weren't very forthcoming with details. It had something to do with human trafficking and prostitution here at the hotel."

Steve broke in. "Heather's worried about the hotel's reputation and how to get ahead of the story if the press gets wind of it. Have either of you heard any rumors about this?"

They looked at each other and shook their heads. "Not me," said Mr. LaPage.

Evie spoke in an emotionless tone. "This has nothing to do with me or my responsibilities. I go from my car to the kitchen and back again. Sorry we couldn't help. Is that all?"

Heather noticed that Evie used a plural pronoun.

"Did it surprise you when Heather said Mr. Malone is in police custody?" asked Steve.

They spoke over each other. Mr. LaPage said yes while Evie said no.

Steve tilted his head. "Why doesn't it surprise you, Ms. Brooks?"

She sputtered, "I don't know. It just doesn't. There's something about him that makes me uncomfortable."

"Did you know him well?"

"No."

"Did he come to the kitchen regularly?"

"He ate like he had a tapeworm." She leaned forward. "He's a body-builder or something like that. I guess activity of that sort requires a lot of calories."

Heather thought back to the pet name the kitchen workers gave Evie Brooks—*Little Miss Sunshine*. The irony couldn't have been more fitting. Evie stood at a strapping five foot nine inches and looked as if she could wrestle a shark and win, but her face would surely crack if she smiled.

In a complete non sequitur, Heather asked, "Ms. Brooks, I couldn't help but notice you're wearing a pair of Allbirds. Mr. LaPage is also wearing a pair. He said he loves his. Are yours as comfortable as they look?"

For the first time Evie smiled, but it flashed and disappeared. "I wouldn't trade them for the world."

Steve changed the subject. "Mr. LaPage, Ms. McBlythe tells me your wife suffers from cancer. How is she?"

The question took the hotel manager by surprise. He covered it by producing a handkerchief and blowing his nose. "Sorry. Allergies." Gathering himself, he said, "We're taking it day by day."

Both Heather and Steve issued a sympathetic nod. Heather drew her eyebrows together. "It surprised me when I checked your personnel file, Mr. LaPage. I noticed your wife isn't covered by the company's health insurance plan. Why is that?"

"Uh... well."

Evie broke in. "I asked the same thing last year. He said she's covered by her employer's plan."

"That makes sense," said Steve, even though it didn't ring true.

Heather came at them from a fresh angle. "This is unpleasant to mention, but the police told me that Mr. Malone made some serious accusations against the two of you."

"I told you, he's a liar," snapped Evie.

"That goes without saying," said Steve. "Still, other members of the board of directors have contacted Heather. They're demanding a full investigation on Malone's activities. Because of his accusations, the police will want to interview both of you. Don't worry, though. We think they'll charge him with murder along with his other crimes."

Heather shook her head. "The board members aren't so sure about the murder. They want Mr. Smiley and me to investigate the murder of Robby Calano." Heather let the words have their effect. "Did you know Mr. Calano is survived by a wife and child?"

Brice LaPage swallowed hard as his head dipped. Evie didn't flinch and issued an unsympathetic, "That's a shame."

Steve remained calm. "Ms. Brooks. You told us a while ago that you only go from your car to your office and back. Do you ever deviate from that routine?"

"Never."

"Where do you park?"

A crack appeared in Evie's hard shell. She responded with a jagged question. "What's that got to do with anything?"

Steve took her reaction in stride. "We were told you park in the VIP garage in the basement."

"Who told you that?" Her gaze danced back and forth. "I bet it was that snake, Malone."

Heather spoke in a soothing tone. "We're contacting everyone who parked in the VIP garage on the day Mr. Calano was killed in hopes someone might have seen something."

Evie leaned forward. "I came to work. I worked all day, and I had to get a ride home. The police wouldn't allow me to get my car until they finished investigating, or gathering evidence, or whatever it is they do."

Heather waited for Steve to confront her with the lie she'd just spoken. With little evidence to process, the forensics crew finished their work by mid-afternoon. The assistant manager had been most insistent in getting the police tape removed as soon as possible. By three in the afternoon, the garage had opened for business.

Instead of confronting her, Steve moved on to another subject. While interviewing he liked to accumulate lies and lay them out like cards when they would do the most damage.

"Have either of you ever heard of a company called B & E Restaurant Supply?" asked Steve.

The pair sitting on the other side of the table looked at each other, shaking their heads in unison. Brice LaPage spoke first. "Is that a company you order from Ms. Brooks?"

Evie looked at Heather. "Perhaps you'd like to examine my records. You won't find an invoice or receipt from a company named B & E. Who are they?"

Heather lifted her shoulders and let them fall. "It's probably a made-up company. It's just that Malone told police that security cameras recorded a truck from B & E as it came to the back dock in the wee hours of the morning."

She didn't tell them which morning. Brice's top lip twitched.

Heather continued. "The driver stayed in the truck. His helper was a scroungy-looking guy wearing a hoody over a Marlin's baseball cap. He cleaned out the walk-in cooler in less than ten minutes."

Mr. LaPage took in a full breath. "Malone will say anything to save his skin. I think he's sending you and the police on a wild-goose chase. I know for a fact that the surveillance cameras in the basement aren't working."

Steve turned his head toward Heather. "That explains it. Didn't you say Malone mentioned someone called Miss Sunshine knows all about the thefts?"

At the mention of her disparaging nickname, Evie's cool gaze turned to ice. A pink hue rose from her chest but stopped at her sun-bronzed face.

It was Heather's turn to go down a different path. "Ms. Brooks, how long have you worked for this hotel?"

"Two years. Why do you ask?"

"Your personnel file is missing." Heather looked at Mr. LaPage. "Can you explain?"

"You need to ask Mr. Cruz. He's been taking care of the lion's share of the personnel issues since Evelyn became ill."

"That's interesting," said Heather. "We spoke to Mr. Cruz earlier, and he told us there are two file cabinets in your office that contain personnel records and that there's a division of labor between the two of you. He takes care of certain departments and you look after the rest, including the kitchen and bookkeeping staff."

The room fell quiet. Heather broke the silence. "I'm ordering a full audit of the hotel and a review of management practices. It looks as though Mr. Cruz may have some serious explaining to do."

Brice LaPage put his hands in his lap and said, "Mr. Cruz has full access to everything in my office. It's been that way since Evelyn got sick."

"How long ago was that?" asked Steve.

His gaze fixed somewhere past Steve, as if he looked into an arduous time of his life. "It started seven years ago."

"That's a long time to deal with something so serious," said Steve. "It reminds me of a case I worked a year or two after I moved to homicide. A guy's wife developed breast cancer. Her illness went on for years before she finally died. That left him saddled with so much debt, he saw no way of ever recovering financially. Then he hit on an idea. He remarried, insured his new bride for several million dollars, and hired a hit man."

Steve concluded with, "It's amazing what a lengthy illness and financial troubles will do to people."

A flash of anger crossed Evie's face. "That's a horrible story to say to someone whose wife is so sick. You owe Mr. LaPage an apology."

Before Steve could answer, Heather's phone sounded a text notification. She glanced down. *Jackpot. Waiting for Vance.* She leaned into Steve. "No need to go on."

Steve folded his hands on the table. "Show them the photograph you took from Mr. LaPage's office this morning."

Heather reached into her briefcase and withdrew a framed photo. "Mr. LaPage, is this a photo of your wife?"

He swallowed hard. "Yes, that's Evelyn. She loved to stand at the rail and watch the ocean slide beneath her."

Heather nodded. "I don't know if I've ever seen such beautiful long blonde hair."

Steve spoke next. "Ms. Brooks, do you like to sail?"

She dipped her head and raised it again. "Yes. Now can we go?"

"Good," said Steve. "A truthful answer at last. So many lies were giving me a headache."

Evie's already narrow gaze intensified. "What are you talking about?"

Steve leaned forward. "We're talking about you and your husband telling one lie after another. We're also talking about a photo displayed in your office with your smiling face on the same sailboat that's in the photo on the table in front of you. Both are photos of you. The one with your hair long he took before you started chemotherapy, and the other, after you completed it.

"It seems B & E Restaurant Supply Company is owned by you, Ms. Brooks." Steve hesitated. "Perhaps I should call you by your married name, Mrs. Evelyn Brooks-LaPage?"

With eyes narrowed to reptilian slits, Evie spoke a two-word challenge. "Prove it."

Her response reminded Heather of a high-stakes poker game where bluffing and bravado sometimes carried the day. Not today. Steve held the winning hand.

"It's not up to us to prove anything. The police are taking care of that little chore, but I'll admit, we told them what to look for."

The game continued with Brice dropping his chin on his chest, a sign he'd folded and wanted out of the game. Evie, however, wasn't about to quit. "They won't find anything because there's nothing to find other than he violated hotel policy by hiring his wife."

Steve roll-tapped his fingers on the desk, starting with his pinkie and progressing to his index finger. "The thing about telling lies is there is usually a thread of truth in them. Brice told us you have cancer. That's at least half true. For years you traveled from Miami to Houston. The hotel you stayed at is near M.D. Anderson, a hospital famous for cancer treatment. We didn't need to get your medical records to piece together you had a lengthy battle which you're now winning."

"So what?" said Evie.

"It occurred to me," said Steve. "That after years of surgeries, chemo and radiation therapy, you might feel cheated by all the money you had to shell out for medical expenses. You felt you got a bum deal with life and realized how brief life can be. You had plans of sailing wherever you wanted and doing it in style. That would take money, big money. You and Brice devised a plan to get it. Hiring you to take care of ordering hotel food supplies was a neat trick. You were well on your way to literally sailing away into the sunset and making up for all the time, pain and money you've been out. Too bad Robbie Calano caught you two in the act."

Steve leaned back. "I'm curious. When did you plan to take all the money you've stolen and leave Miami in that fancy sailboat?"

Evie sprung from her seat. In her right hand she held a pistol, small, but the business end looked plenty big to do the job.

They hadn't counted on Evie having this ace up her sleeve.

36

Further discussion turned out to be short, and one sided. Heather and Steve were to lead the way out of the hotel, acting as a shield to Evie.

"Get behind us," commanded Evie to her husband. She stood behind him, menacing with the pistol.

"It's no use. They know everything."

"You're such a coward," snapped Evie. She brought the pistol down hard behind his ear, driving him to the carpet. She then fixed her gaze on Heather. "Stand up. Both of you."

Steve and Heather rose at the same time. He unfurled his cane and said, "At least we now know it was you that shot Robby. Brice didn't have the guts."

"Shut up and drop the stick," said Evie. "She can guide you."

Steve's cane fell to the floor with a rattle. "When did you suspect we knew?"

"When you asked about the shoes."

Steve's words came out calm, measured and mocking. "Next time you want to murder someone, don't wear shoes with the tops made of wool. Blood gets into the fibers and it's next to impossible to get it out. I'm confident the police will find traces of Robby's blood despite how much you may have cleaned them."

Heather added, "They should have the delivery van in custody by now. We're betting the blood in it matches Robby's, too."

Evie nudged Heather in the ribs with her pistol. "I'm not planning on being around for a trial. My boat is packed and ready to sail. I've had a concealed-carry permit for a long time, and I know how to use this thing. I don't leave the house without my little friend."

Steve snickered. "Little friend? You've been watching too many movies. Don't you know the crooks never get away?"

"Shut up, blind man."

The barrel pressed more firmly against Heather's back. "That's a cute little gun. Is it a Glock 42?"

"Wrong," said Evie. She walked so close that Heather could feel warm breaths on her neck. "It's a Glock 43, not a 42."

Steve said, "Let me guess... you got the model with the pink grip."

"That's the one," said Heather. "Six shots, .9mm."

This wasn't good. The semi-automatic could deliver three chunks of lead each into her and Steve before either could react.

"Shut up and walk. Stop when I tell you to."

Evie moved them toward the door and gave instructions to place their noses against the wall. Steve said, "There's an officer waiting for us to come out."

"He won't let us pass," added Heather. "You might as well give up."

A voice alive with hatred said, "Take off your coat, blind man."

Steve slipped out of his navy jacket. Evie took it and draped it over her right wrist, concealing the short-barreled pistol. "Here's what you're going to do: Fancy lady is on the blind guy's left. I'll be on his right with my pistol pointed at his ribs. If either of you tries to get cute, he'll join that nosy chef in the morgue. I want you both to walk past the cop. Don't say a word and take a left when we get to the main hallway."

"That won't work," said Steve. "We can't walk past that cop without speaking. He'll know something is up."

Heather wondered what Steve's plan was.

"I'll tell him your husband confessed, and he needs to place him in handcuffs," said Steve.

The plan stunned Evie into silence. She took long seconds to mull over her choices. "All right. You tell him, but if you're not convincing, your white shirt will be a red mess."

The officer hesitated when Heather told him he needed to arrest the hotel manager. She reassured him Detective Warner authorized it. That did the trick. He hustled to the classroom door and went in with pistol drawn.

"Smart move," said Evie. "Keep going to the fishing exhibition. When we get there, we're walking down the center aisle like nothing's wrong. The doors along the back wall lead outside to a parking lot where boats and trailers are on display. So are a lot of shiny new trucks to pull them with. Once we get outside, I'll convince someone to loan us a truck."

"Not bad," said Steve. "There's only a couple hundred things that can go wrong."

"Shut up! You talked me into one of your schemes. I'm taking over from here."

Steve shrugged. "Just trying to keep you alive long enough for you to go to prison."

Heather tried to slow the pace around the Christmas trees studding the hallway, but Evie would have none of it. The threats continued.

Steve chimed in. "It's not her fault. If you hadn't made me leave my cane, I'd be making better time."

Heather stole a glance over her shoulder, hoping to see Detective Warner. Not good. If the cavalry didn't come before they entered the exhibition hall, it could be a real mess. A crowded room, a loaded pistol, and a desperate murderess made a recipe for disaster.

The entrance of the fishing show came into view. A pair of women dressed alike stood at the door checking wristbands for patrons and credentials for vendors. Heather had to think of something fast.

37

———

The two women looked like smiling bookends. Tall, with mahogany-colored skin, they greeted the trio with a warmth worthy of their Bahamian accents. The one nearest Evie said, "If you goin' to the fish expo, you need a ticket."

Heather grimaced. Would Evie unveil the pistol and start shooting? Instead, she spoke in an authoritative voice. "I'm Ms. Brooks, a supervisor for the hotel. I need to check the food vendors to make sure they're meeting hygiene standards."

The two women looked at each other. Their expressions told Heather the gatekeepers weren't convinced.

"Do you know Bella Brumley?" asked Steve.

Smiles made the skin around the two women's eyes furrow. "She's giving a demonstration."

The second one said, "I think every fisherman from Orlando to the Keys came to see her."

Steve followed up his original question with, "Did you read the book of her life?"

"Uh, huh," said the one nearest Steve. "Can't wait to see the movie."

Heather joined in. "Do you remember the blind detective and his attorney partner?"

"Lord have mercy, you them!"

Steve issued a toothy smile. "Bella invited us to come this morning. She said she'd have tickets waiting for us."

Both women reached for a door handle and pulled. The one nearest Heather said, "You better hurry. She been at it a while."

Once inside the door, Evie said, "So far, you've been lucky. Now's not the time to get cute. Walk straight down the aisle and don't talk to anyone."

Booths displayed everything imaginable related to the fishing industry. Tanned men and women wearing bright clothing with logos gave practiced sales pitches. Like an army of ants, patrons moved from one glitzy display to the next.

"I hear Bella," said Steve as he walked at a slow, steady pace. He kept a soft grip on Heather's shoulder as she blazed the trail through the crowd.

"I see her," said Heather. "She's high on a platform overlooking what looks like a giant aquarium."

"Keep walking and shut up," said Evie in a harsh whisper.

A tightly packed crowd gathered around the demonstration pool set back from the center aisle. The plexiglass sides rose eight feet above a five-foot-tall base, giving the crowd an unobstructed view of the blue-green water.

From her high perch, Bella cast a lure to the far end of the tank. It landed a few inches shy of a tree stump and stayed on top of the water. She cranked the handle of the reel, drawing the zig-zagging lure toward her. All the while she explained how it worked to drive fish into a feeding frenzy by creating vibrations that mimicked a bait fish. The crowd applauded as she pulled the lure from the water and snipped it free from the line. Bending over, she reached for another shiny object in a tackle box. That's when Bella caught Heather's gaze.

Heather shook her head as vigorously as she dared. Luckily, Steve stood between her and Evie. Heather mouthed the word GUN. She followed it with HELP!

The last thing Heather saw of Bella was her tying the lure she'd retrieved to a fishing line.

Bella's voice sounded over speakers set up around the display. "The next bait I'll show you is a real winner. This is a sinking twitch-bait. As you can see, it's three inches long, has a silver body with dark gray spots, three treble hooks, and a red face. The shiny eyes are so real you'll think she's winking at you when you tie her on your line."

The crowd issued a laugh on cue.

"Like I told you," said Bella. "This is a sinking lure. You need to let it drop, then reel it in with a smooth, even motion. Occasionally you'll want to give the tip of your rod a light twitch."

Bella took a deep breath and continued. "I'll need everyone's help when I cast this. I want you to shout *Get Down!* when I tell you to. Can you do that for me?"

Steve whispered to Heather, "Ready?"

"Ready for what?"

The doors to the parking lot and Evie's escape stood mere yards away. Behind them, Detective Warner's voice boomed. "Police! Stop!"

"Get down!" shouted Bella, followed by a chorus of anglers giving the same command.

Steve fell to the ground, taking his coat with him. Evie spun to meet the threat posed by Detective Warner. Heather threw herself over Steve, looking up at Evie as she did. A whizzing sound, like a bee in flight, filled the air.

Evie's gun hand shot upward to shield her face. What looked like a silver blur wrapped around her wrist. Her arm jerked toward the casting exhibition and she let out a shriek. The pistol fell and bounced on the carpet. Robby Calano's killer went to her knees, bellowing in pain. Her right hand jerked as if it had a mind of its own as she reached for the pistol with her left hand.

Bella stood on the platform some twenty-five yards away, the tip of her rod bent to form a C.

Heather sprung from her position of covering Steve. She took a single, long step and unleashed a kick to Evie's belly. A whoosh came forth, leaving Evie gasping.

Detective Warner arrived and pinned Evie to the carpet with a knee between her shoulder blades. Detective Vance pocketed the pistol after he placed it in a plastic evidence bag. Warner freed the lure from the fishing line with a lock-blade knife. Amid screams of pain, invectives, and threats, Vance and Warner pulled Evie's hands behind her, taking care not to impale themselves with the few remaining barbs not sunk deep into Evie's bloody wrist.

Vance looked up. "I'll need you two and Bella to come with us." He grimaced as he rose to his feet. "Thanks for the help. This collar might be enough to keep me around a while longer."

Bella arrived just as Steve reached a standing position. Fully enfolded in his arms, she hugged until he convinced her he'd escaped unharmed. Their hands stayed linked until Evie's screaming threats faded away and Steve said, "I'm starving. Let's find a pizza."

"Not so fast," said Heather. "Someone's pushing through the crowd to talk to you."

"Me?" asked Steve.

The answer came when Kate's arms wrapped around him. She whispered before she pulled away, "I brought your cane." She added, "One thousand and thirty-nine mystery writers are on pins and needles. I need to get back and tell them you're all right."

The afternoon clicked by at a much slower pace. Detectives took statements, and all who wanted to partake ate pizza off paper plates in Detective Warner's office, which amounted to a cubicle in a warren of cops. Steve and Heather knew the routine and how long it would take.

"What time is it?" asked Steve as they arrived back at the hotel.

"Ten after five," replied Heather.

"Let's hope we're not too late."

"I'm hoping Latrice put together a video of the security footage."

38

"Go straight to the stage," said Steve.

Kate met them as they scaled the last step. "I'm not sure how much longer I can hold them off."

"Let Heather and me have a crack at them."

Even though Steve couldn't see her, Kate made a sweeping motion with her hand to show the room belonged to them.

Standing side by side behind the podium, Steve and Heather remained silent until the room quieted. Heather leaned toward the microphone. "We apologize for not being able to come and discuss the interviewing techniques we demonstrated this morning, but we've been a little tied up solving five cases."

Steve added, "Not as tied up as Malone, Evie Brooks, and Brice LaPage."

The quip got the intended result as some laughed and others nodded in affirmation.

Heather made a quarter turn toward him. "At least you didn't say they went down, *hook, line and sinker.*"

A groan came from Steve and many in the crowd. Not to be outdone, he said, "Before we sail into the uncharted waters of terrible clichés, let's drop anchor and ask our attendees if it surprised them when Evie Brooks pulled out that cute little pistol."

"Aye, aye, captain," said Heather with a two-fingered salute as she turned and faced the crowd. "How many of you thought Steve and I were goners when Evie marched us out at gunpoint?"

At least half the room raised their hands.

"How many of you thought it was part of a play, something we made up?"

The rest raised their hands.

Steve then asked, "Perhaps you'd like to see what happened after Evie Brooks took us hostage and tried to make her escape."

A screen unrolled from the ceiling behind the stage as the lights dimmed. Edited security footage gave an almost continuous account of Steve and Heather's trek with Evie Brooks' pink pistol discretely covered by Steve's jacket. The account played on, switching from one security camera to the next as it recorded everything from the abduction until police led Evie away in handcuffs.

The house lights came back on and Heather waited for people to stop blinking and the rumble of voices to still.

At a microphone in the center aisle Elissa stood with arms folded.

Heather acknowledged her presence with a nod. "I'm sure you have questions about the interview and subsequent events. However, let me assure you that the murder of Robby Calano really happened at this hotel and the pistol is real. It is now in police evidence."

Not waiting to be recognized, Elissa spoke with the voice of a practiced politician. "I'm sure I speak for every member when I say how impressed we are with the skill and courage both of you displayed, and I'd like our members to show our appreciation."

It took a while for the applause to die down. Elissa spoke over the last claps. "Ms. McBlythe, you said earlier that you and Mr. Smiley have been busy solving five cases since you arrived.

By my count, you still have two unaccounted for. Kira Kelly and Lara Lovejoy."

Steve said, "Ms. Lutz has wasted no time in asking about a matter of concern since before this convention started. It's a fair question and one that deserves an answer, but not before I set the stage. After all, this is a mystery writers' convention, and a mystery remains."

The room fell quiet as an empty church.

"Let me begin with Kira," said Steve. "She's described as a talented, independent author who kept abreast of the latest technologies. She stayed on the cutting edge of all trends and championed writers who want to publish their works and receive the full fruits of their labors." He paused. "Is that an accurate description, Elissa?"

The former model unfurled her arms and said, "You might mention she's a best-selling author and a gifted teacher who gives her time away to anyone who asks." Elissa pulled her teeth over her bottom lip and continued. "Unlike some, she's not afraid to embrace change and she possesses all that's necessary to drag this organization into today's reality."

Murmurs arose from the traditional writers, but Steve spoke over them. "What you don't know is at Wednesday's happy hour and mixer, Heather and I received three requests to investigate Kira's disappearance. The requests came from Elissa Lutz, Hazel Smallgrass, and Kate Bridges. Since we only represent one client at a time, we chose the middle ground and went with Kate, a hybrid author."

Taking a step forward, Heather added, "I hope everyone sees how odd it was that we'd get three identical requests in one afternoon. Also, two of the three women requesting our services had already hired private detectives who'd come up blank. We subsequently received two reports and Steve reviewed them carefully."

"I'll have more to say about those in a little while," said Steve.

"But first, let me backtrack and talk about Lara Lovejoy. She stood behind me when we checked in and I had a brief conversation with her. I found her to be shy, but engaging all the same. It came as a surprise when I heard she was being groomed to run for president of this organization until I learned of her exceptional talent and quiet way of getting things done behind the scenes."

Steve moved a half step to the side, giving Heather her cue to take over. "I reviewed the security tapes after Ms. Lovejoy checked in. She came with only a carry-on bag and her purse. She went to a restaurant in the atrium following check in and disappeared. We believe she must have gone through the kitchen to a back door that leads to hallways used by staff, and eventually to stairways not covered by cameras."

Holding up his index and middle fingers, Steve spoke. "Two well-respected authors, two candidates for president and two mysterious disappearances. In both cases, neither we nor the police found any evidence of foul play." Steve held out his arms with palms exposed. "Where did Kira and Lara go?"

A sliver of a smile gave away how much he enjoyed this moment. Like a cat playing with a mouse, Steve had the room pinned to their seats even though he couldn't see their faces. He dropped his hands. "We found Lara and Kira and I'll give you a clue that will help you discover how. Our research showed that Kira and Lara never attended past conventions at the same time. When you think you might know the answer to these two disappearances, come to the microphone."

No one moved until a slender woman with reading glasses perched on the end of her nose came forth from the back of the room. A second woman, much younger, with multiple piercings in her ears and bottom lip came and stood beside Elissa, waiting her turn.

Contestant number one cleared her throat. "This reminds me of one of Hazel's early books, Double-Trouble Murder. Non-identical twin sisters gave each other alibis throughout the story, including when they took turns stabbing their stepmother, who'd poisoned their father."

Steve nodded. "Are you saying Kira and Lara are twins, or at least lookalikes?"

Heads shook in disagreement, followed by voices saying, "They look and act differently." Another shouted, "One was an Indie and the other a trad. There's no way."

Steve held his palms up to quiet the room. "That's a good guess, but it's not correct. Kira and Lara are not sisters." He paused. "Who else thinks they've solved the case?"

"I'm a psychology major," said the second woman. "The only way this makes sense is if there's only one woman with two distinct personalities. I've read of such cases and I'm sure we've all heard of multiple personality disorder. It's rare that she took it to such an extreme, but Lara and Kira have to be the same person. I hope you've found her. She'll need extensive therapy."

"Are you saying that anyone who assumes the role of another person needs counseling and will most likely require psychiatric intervention?" asked Steve. "What about actors? What about children play-acting? What about a person who dresses up in a Santa Claus outfit at Christmas?"

"Well—"

Steve didn't let her finish. "Cops dress in all kinds of disguises to catch criminals, and the bad guys aren't averse to altering their appearances. In fact, people of all kinds change their looks for legitimate and even noble causes."

"Are you saying I'm wrong?" asked the woman with her hands on her hips and her blue hair shimmering.

Steve issued a sly smile. "Neither you nor the first woman to speak are completely wrong, but neither of you have the full picture."

Heather put her hand on Steve's shoulder. "You've had your fun. Tell them." She took two steps back and three to the side.

Turning a quarter turn, Steve extended his hand to Kate and

asked her to join him. When she arrived at his side he asked, "Do you want to tell them or should I?"

Kate scanned the room. She placed her left hand on the podium and, with it blocking the sight of her clasping Steve's hand, she announced, "I'm Kira Kelly, Lara Lovejoy and Kate Bridges."

Gasps rose, as did words of unbelief. Eyes squinted to see the resemblance between Kate and the two women she pretended to be. Elissa's open-jawed expression matched that of many who tried to bridge the gap between what they knew of three different women who were now a single person in front of them.

For proof, Kate donned a wig, put on a plain sweater, buttoned it to the top, rolled her shoulders forward, slumped, and spoke with the meek voice of Lara Lovejoy. "I could just as easily put on my other wig, change clothes, and you'd be looking at Kira Kelly."

Steve quickly added, "She's absolutely devoted to this organization and everything she's done is for its benefit. Listen closely and she'll explain." He took several steps back.

Alone now, with hands clasping the edges of the podium, Kate lifted her chin. "I could see the division coming years ago, and I devised a plan to bridge the gap between tradition and innovation. Time will tell if the plan works or not."

Her head dipped as she joined her hands together as if to pray and looked about the crowd. "There's not a woman alive I loved more than Hazel, and I'm grieving her loss as much as I grieved my mother's." She looked into the faces of the writers. "Most of you do not understand how she poured herself into the art and craft of writing and helping others to succeed. Yet, she was a product of generations of traditional writers, agents, editors and publishers. Age, declining heath and change conspired to overwhelm her until all she had left was her spirt and pride. That, and the fear of being left without purpose."

Giving the crowd a soft smile, Kate lifted her voice. "I could see what Hazel could not. Things needed to change. Lara

Lovejoy is the name I originally published under, and I still crank out two books a year under that name. She's the shy, plain woman Hazel molded into a star of the mystery genre. But there was another woman wanting to break out and into something new and exciting. What better place to reinvent myself, and this organization, than from the inside? Enter Kira Kelly, the independent writer with an avant-garde hair do, trendy clothes and stories for a younger audience."

Elissa's strained voice bellowed, "You're a fake!"

Steve took quick steps to the podium. "Kate Bridges is not a fake, nor does she think like you, Elissa. Things are not always right or wrong, my way or no way. Everything she's done has been for the good of this organization. She's trying to sew the past to the future in ways you don't know or care about."

Steve swung his hand over the crowd. "Look around you, Elissa. Count the number of traditional and hybrid writers. Why can't there be room for all mystery writers in this organization?"

Compassion filled Kate's voice as she looked at Elissa. "Steve's right. I believe with all my heart there's room for both. That's why I formed a third persona." She cast her gaze to the entire room. "I need to confess that Kate Bridges is my true name. I had deep personal reasons involving abuse and fear for my life when I began writing under the name Lara Lovejoy. Kira Kelly came along when I realized independent writing and publishing could be a viable alternative to people with a heart for writing but didn't want to follow a traditional path."

Steve stayed by Kate's side. "If you take the time to do a little research, you'll find that Lara Lovejoy and Kate Bridges have the same agent, editors and publisher. Also, Kira Kelly and Kate Bridges publish their independent books under the imprint of Kira's company name."

Kate looked at Steve. "Is that how you figured out I'm all three?"

"That only confirmed it." said Steve. "Lara and Kate wore the same perfume the first day we met."

Kate looked at the group from left to right. "This is interesting." She turned back to Steve. "What other clues did you have?"

"The reports from the private detectives made me suspicious."

"How so? I did extensive research. I'm sure I nailed the terminology, the standard fees and how PI's interact with the police."

"It wasn't any of that," said Steve. "I took a course in creative writing in college. Although most of it didn't stay with me, I remember something a professor said about what sets exceptional writers apart from others. It's the author's voice. I listened to both reports four or five times before I realized the same person wrote them, and that person had the same voice as the woman who writes mysteries I've enjoyed for years."

"You could identify my voice in dry reports from two made-up PIs?"

Steve issued a coy smile. "It helped when they didn't return my calls."

A petulant voice interrupted as Elissa spoke into the microphone again. "We need to move on. When are we going to take nominations for president?"

Steve spoke up. "Before we came to this morning's session, I submitted my application and payment for membership in this organization. I may be new, but according to the bylaws, any member can submit nominations for president. I nominate Kate Bridges as president."

A chorus of voices seconded the motion.

Steve stood back as Kate asked for other nominations. Elissa tried to catch the eye of several of her disciples, but each averted their gaze.

Thirty seconds doesn't sound like a long time, but it must have felt that way to Elissa as no one put forth her name.

Elissa lifted her chin, put on her best I-don't-care expression and gave her last runway walk of the day. The shouts of electing

Kate as president by acclimation must have been the ultimate insult as Elissa escaped the room.

Heather led Steve down the steps and placed him in a chair as Kate informed the crowd she'd announce the rest of the officers at the night's banquet.

Heather met her at the bottom step after she'd dismissed the group. "We need to talk."

Kate pulled her close and whispered. "I've been thinking the same thing. I'll call you as soon as I get to my room."

39

P lates and silverware rattled and clanked as servers removed the last vestiges of the night's banquet, except Steve's second cup of coffee. Kate patted his hand as she rose. "Wish me luck."

He did and Bella whispered, "She looks amazing, no more worry lines around her eyes and mouth."

Steve replied with a nod.

Speakers popped as Kate flipped the switch on the microphone. She sounded poised and deftly gave a moving tribute to Hazel that included a short montage of photos cataloguing the history of the former president from when she first held a gavel until last year's awards banquet.

A series of awards followed, culminating in the coveted "Mystery Writer of the Year Award," which, ironically, went to the one person who chose not to attend, Elissa. Kate made up for the awkwardness of the moment by saying, "I'll make sure Elissa gets this and that she knows what an asset she is to this organization. There's no way I'll lose her when she has so much to offer."

Steve swiveled in his chair and reached for his water glass but didn't have time to raise it.

"At this time," said Kate. "I'd like Steve Smiley, Heather McBlythe and Bella Brumley to come to the stage."

Steve found Bella's wrist. "What have you and Heather been up to?"

"I dunno," responded Bella as if she hadn't a clue.

"As they're making their way," said Kate. "We promised you these three will sign copies of Bella's runaway bestselling memoir. The hotel has purchased copies for all attendees and there's no need to rush. They'll stay as long as necessary."

With a hand on Bella's shoulder, Steve climbed while Kate continued speaking. "Before you form a line, I have one more announcement to make. I want to follow Hazel's example of mentoring undiscovered writers. I also want to incorporate the latest technology and reach as wide an audience as possible. To accomplish this, I'll be working with our newest member, Mr. Steve Smiley. Ms. McBlythe and I are still working out the details but I'll be sharing her townhome over the holidays, which adjoins Mr. Smiley's. If any members want to take part in a daily interactive session with me and Mr. Smiley, there's a sign up on the website. We'll broadcast each daily episode live on YouTube. If you can't make the live broadcasts, please catch up at your convenience.

"Mr. Smiley doesn't know it yet, but he has eighteen books on craft to absorb before I temporarily move from Florida, and we begin the week before Christmas. The course and my stay in Texas will last three weeks."

Kate issued a smile, then lifted her voice a third of an octave. "If you'd like an autographed copy of Bella's book, please make your way to the stage."

Bella deposited Steve in a chair and sat beside him. He whispered, "What if I don't want to become a writer?"

"You'll either learn to write or Kate will play Christmas music at full volume."

Steve beckoned Bella to share a secret. "Can anyone hear us?"

"Heather and Kate are opening boxes of books."

"I decided to start writing on the flight from Houston to Miami. I wasn't sure how to start, but my plan came together, if I do say so myself. Don't tell Heather or Kate. I want them to think this is all their idea."

Thank you for reading *Pistols And Poinsettias*. I hope you enjoyed your holiday escape as you turned the pages to find out whodunit! If you loved it, please consider leaving a review at your favorite retailer, Bookbub or Goodreads. Your reviews help other readers discover their next great mystery!

To stay abreast of Smiley and McBlythe's latest adventure, and all my book news, join my Mystery Insiders community. As a thank you, I'll send you a reader exclusive Smiley and McBlythe mystery novella.

You can also follow me on Amazon, Bookbub and Goodreads to receive notification of my latest release.

Happy reading!
Bruce

Scan the image above or go to brucehammack.com/the-smiley-and-mcblythe-mysteries-prequel.

An inheritance worth millions. A killer with a list... and Smiley's on it.

Blind PI Smiley's job as executor of a large Texas estate is complicated by the rancher's suspicious death. While the sheriff is investigating the rancher's death, the ranch foreman is found murdered.

Smiley begins his executor duties and quickly realizes any of the four siblings could be guilty of one, or both, of the murders. There's no love lost in the dysfunctional family. But which one wanted the land bad enough to kill for it? Or was it a conspiracy?

When Smiley is hired by the foreman's family to find the killer, his investigation unearths a long-buried family secret that could solve the mystery, but will it also lead to more killing? Steve needs to stop the killer or the next funeral could be his.

Scan below to get your copy of *Five Card Murder*.

brucehammack.com/books/five-card-murder/